The Book of Ruth

ALSO BY FRANK LENTRICCHIA

Fiction
Lucchesi and The Whale
The Music of the Inferno
Johnny Critelli and The Knifemen

Memoir
The Edge of Night

Nonfiction
Crimes of Art and Terror (with Jody McAuliffe)
Modernist Quartet
Ariel and the Police
Criticism and Social Change
After the New Criticism
Robert Frost
The Gaiety of Language

As Editor
Dissent From the Homeland
Close Reading: The Reader (with Andrew DuBois)
Introducing Don DeLillo
New Essays on "White Noise"
Critical Terms for Literary Study
Robert Frost: A Bibliography

The Book of Ruth

A Novel

by Frank Lentricchia

Ravenna Press · Seattle 2005

© 2005 Frank Lentricchia
All rights reserved
Printed in the United States of America
Typeset in Officina Serif by TypeRight, Inc.
LCCN 2005901978 ● ISBN 0-9766593-5-2

Second Printing

Just for Maeve

The Book of Ruth

I

Ninth Lake

Fall, 2002

Sleep-deprived and staggered, melancholy Lucchesi says aloud to no one, because no one is there, not even himself, "I am hopelessly old," as he searches the bathroom mirror for the face he never had—dwelling without mercy on the unacceptable image, touching the evidence of deterioration, who has only Ruth now to save him from himself—Ruth, his grieving wife, who grieves because her erratic husband has told her too many times that there can be no joy, no intimacy, no refuge, nothing at all for Thomas Lucchesi, Junior, except inside the art of his fiction.

In the desert of his cabin, Lucchesi mourns for Lucchesi. Junior: The word repeats in the delicate ear of his mind, saying exactly that which he wants to hear, and so he scrawls it everywhere: at the upper left-hand corner of envelopes, without fail; on his checks and all documents—including legal instruments—that require his signature, though his birth certificate verifies no such identification; on the title pages of the numerous unpublished manuscripts of his experimental novels, for which he has long since ceased to seek publication, so lovingly he scrawls it. He thinks and writes "Junior" now more than ever because at seventy-one it whispers to him, the self-panderer, that his body has not changed (not that much, really, depending on the lighting), that his father, who has been dead for thirty-four years, and with whom his relationship was emotionally desiccated from the start, is still alive. That he's not next.

Lucchesi fears many things, including Ruth, most especially Ruth, in whom he has nevertheless invested the power to cure what he calls, in the literary rhetoric he delights to cultivate in times of crisis, "this long disease, my life." To be cured by Ruth, to be cured for happiness. But what is that? What is happiness? He wants an answer.

He tells her that he loves her. Not a day goes by when he doesn't. More than once she'd responded, "No forcing, Lucky!" He's told her that his consuming need is to "fabricate from our passion an intimate life, and thereby to yield myself to something larger and more valuable than myself." Said to a woman he married twelve years ago. And she replied, deadpan, "Yes, let's do that. Let's do it soon." A week ago he had written a love note, but could not give it to her, because he was afraid. "To annihilate myself in the consuming fire of your flesh—I, a dried up, puny stick of a writer." He feared the impiety of her laughter (no gods for Ruth), even as he understood its benevolence, because Ruth is benevolence itself. Such an absurdity: fear of a benevolent wife. He understands the absurdity, still he withholds—holds himself, rather than Ruth, tightly. Ruth, who bows to nothing and nobody, including this man she loves with a commitment that defies description, this man she fears has sealed himself away forever inside the tomb of his art.

In the dead quiet of his cabin, Lucchesi sucks the icy dark of his desire to write and drops his pajama bottoms. Asquat the throne of his brooding contemplation, he poses a question, mumbles it with shame (a hopeful sign, his shame), "Does Junior love Ruth?" while avoiding the one question that matters: Can Lucchesi love, or is he just another artist, one more specialist in first degree murder of the spirit? Ruth's spirit to be precise. His too in the process.

He wipes. Checks the paper. Blood. Frank, and more than a little. Colon cancer. No doubt. He flushes, rises hoisting his bottoms, thinking, In this house I'm in solitary confinement. Smiles a little, this time not out of the usual lacerating self-pity. This time out of an uncorroded glimpse of reality. Another hopeful sign, though the idea of Lucchesi and the idea of hope can be conjoined only with the greatest difficulty. He'll go to Ruth, that's what he'll do, who doesn't live in his cabin.

Steps out of his bottoms. Removes his top. One last terrified glance in the mirror, *then I'll go to Ruth*. The murderous mirror: He'd better go to Ruth.

❂

He can't help himself, it's an addiction, this persistent mythifying of her, so that when she fails him, in the banal minor ways of human failure, he loses his grip, how easily he loses his grip on the belief that she actually loves him without qualification and will never abandon him, and then he's sucked down into the black hole of chronic depression. Her words do no good. "I love you" does no good. And then this man who fears death night and day looks forward to it, because he does not believe with belief's full fantastic strength, no longer believes what he had believed to be true, what he says he believes when he tells Ruth too often that he believes her, he who has so little strength for Ruth and is constantly on highest alert for her every lapse from perfection. He who has the gravest difficulty believing that she loves him.

If asked if she had ever betrayed or failed him in the gut-stabbing ways of intimate relationships, he would be forced to answer, being an honest man, in the negative. If asked what difference his negative response would make to his assessment of his despair, he would answer, quickly, none. And so he continues to file away the evidence for future consultation, he files it in the nearly impregnable fortress of his resentment, and in his bed, his sleepless bed, picks through it like a hungry raccoon rummaging in a garbage bin. Lucchesi has no faith: not in Ruth, not in himself, not in his art, not in God. What is God? This man, who so fears death and disfiguration, doles out a little of both, periodically, to the woman he calls his wife. Doles out much, and ceaselessly, to himself, especially when in the throes of his recurrent bouts of jealousy, which he's convinced are both irremediable and groundless.

The striking figure opening the door of the cabin is a solid six-footer, with no trace of stoop and only minimal thickening at the waist—a v-shaped specimen of manhood still, to whom his forty-eight-year-old internist had recently remarked in amazement, when he pulled off his t-shirt, that he, the ruddy Lucchesi, with the well-toned pectorals, had not yet yielded to gravity, would apparently never yield, to which the patient replies: "The composed and contented man is far less subject to nature's relentless narrative; I am such a man, am I not?"

Except for the handsomely retreated hairline, it's all there in crew cut silver gray, and he's still apple-hard above the mouth, advanced age attacking the face only moderately with loose skin along the jaw-line and at the throat, though doubtless attacking his body in other ways as well, in places at this time indiscernible even to the fearful instruments of medical science—though eventually to be discerned.

What is possible for him to know is that he is a lucky man ("No forcing, Lucky!"), that at seventy-one his age remains almost irrelevant, if he would permit himself to know and embrace what he has never known and embraced, will likely never know and never embrace in the brief time he has left, the lucky physical truth of himself, a seventy-one-year streak of unbroken good luck.

Here he comes now from the darkness of his cabin into the earliest light, moving with urgent intent toward Ruth, who is not a myth, *Ruth*, moving briskly through the fifteen yards (a safe distance) that separate his cabin from hers. The wind off the lake— a moonlit mirror—is chilly. The cabins, set up on a rise and back from the rocky shore's edge, but not far back, are weathered white by time's infinite course. White flowers front the cabins, the flowers a little dried, their white less white than it used to be. Lucchesi stops, turns and looks blankly back at his dark and empty place, *myself am blanched*, as the wind blows a fine, cruel grit hard against his face and bare arms and this extremist feels the change of season toward ice and solitude, and he is afraid. Turns back abruptly toward her cabin, where there is light—quick quick now. Knocks. No response. Opens the door. She's gone.

Repeatedly jolted awake at 1:00, 3:00, and 5:00 a.m., in need of consolation in his lonely bed, he does not listen for the transcendent lamentations of loons. He'll not be granted the pleasure of loons, because there are no loons. Three decades of acid rain render this lake in New York's Adirondack mountains breathtakingly crystalline, and fishless.

Imagine the scene from a point off shore and over the water—as if you were standing on a platform, its pilings sunk deep and secured on bedrock, the platform built to meet the single implacable need of a serious photographer. The platform is real. It is Ruth's place. The scene is composed of the two cabins, there are no others, the unavoidable rocky shore, the fading white flowers, and the dark pines that back the whitened cabins tightly and grow to the water's edge along the entire course of the lake's shoreline, except here in this small half-circle hacked out for habitation—hacked out and periodically re-hacked to kill off the seedlings and ever re-emergent brush that would heal the wound.

The scene is flecked, but not much leavened, by recurrent occasions of the human: a man sitting in a metal folding chair at the water's edge, reading or staring, mostly staring; or faced up on a cool day, eyes closed, into the blessing of the sun, because the sick believe that they get well fast in the sun; or sitting there asleep, in rain gear, in a storm; or huddled into himself, outfitted for winter weather, under the frigid brilliance of a hard January sky, taking notes; or standing before his cabin, back to water, arms akimbo, in reverie, focused on the cabin wall, inches from the wall, then darting between the cabins, so often darting between, or halted midway, too often halted midway, too often turning back, head down, shoulders slumped; or lounging in his doorway (this is rare), leaning and uncurling a hand in sweet greeting, the smile is vulnerable, to someone on the platform we do not yet see, then for comic relief doing the donkey, jackass that he is, thumbs in ears and fingers flapping (last trace of his Neapolitan inheritance) to the loved one on the platform; or naked, white-bodied and ghostly, except for the ruddy face, dancing in the snow (more often than you'd guess); or standing, as he now stands, backlit, darkly figured in her doorway.

The unseen presence behind every image is Ruth Cohen. Ruth is real. This scene and its occasional human fleckings constitute her severe subject, the end of her photographic art, and her last project: a variable man pursued across the hours of light and dark.

From the Platform

After twelve years of gentle love he turns at the sink and throws the big fork hard against the wall behind me. Not a word, nothing. Later, in the dark, he's in my arms and still breathing hard, and I say, That was wonderful, do you want to say something? Nothing. So I say, Put this in your mouth, and he does, because he likes everything I make him do in the dark. We lie quiet for a long time. Then he says, It's my so-called life as a writer, it's that aggressive moron in Washington D.C. No, I say, it's not the writing and it's not the moron. It's your resentment. It's your fear, which you call jealousy. It's only fear. Put your finger in, put it deep, and I'll steal away all of your fear and all of your resentment—let me steal away all of your thoughts. He does it tenderly, he kisses me, and then he says, his finger still in, It's your past in Cuba, that's what it is, and the circles you moved in after Cuba. Those famous men of Camelot. The thought makes me feel alone and small. Powerful and dashing men before me, whom you found cosmopolitan and witty. That's what it is. Sexy men before me. I do not respond. He's still in my arms. You fucked them. I imagine scenes in vivid detail. That's what it is. I say, I'm here. I'm here now. You're here. Are you here? Shall I do something special for you? I want to do something special for you. Nothing, again nothing. His finger still in. I say, Your silence is worse than the big fork in the throat. He says, Since there's no help, come let us kiss and part. He laughs, in a certain way. Some poet in his mind, as usual. I won't respond. He says, My life stands as a loaded gun. And this is how he escapes me, with words that come from writing. I couldn't say, How can you feel alone with me here, and your finger in me wet, unless you actually don't love me, because I know that he does. Instead I say, I know a miracle cure for your literary tongue. Would you like to take the cure now? Speak to me. Speak. Can you not speak? I can't tell if he's smiling in the dark. I say, I love you, Thomas. Accept my love. He gets up and says, I'm sorry. Please forgive me. I love you, Ruth. Then he leaves and I'm in my empty bed.

I need an art mute and cold—like a fish at the bottom of the North Sea.

✺

He's frozen at the threshold of her cabin, staring into the absence within, when he hears the canoe bump the shore and suddenly Ruth in the water—full-bodied in cut offs, sweatshirt, and a Yankees cap, camera case slung over her shoulder—a tall redhead at fifty-eight going slowly blond, an ex-tennis player with a very big serve, hauling the canoe up so easily onto the rack.

Granted, less impulsive, less the genius of the moment than she used to be, when long ago she'd gotten illegally into Havana in the bad period just before the Missile Crisis, a few days before the blockade, and had hit the streets there without a plan, only desire, desire without an object, her mind an unexposed film. Yet somehow the right ones had found her, she told *The New Yorker*, because they could not bear anymore to be mysterious, there was so little time. They wanted this college senior with such a smile of sunshine to smile with your camera on us, *bonita*, see how we have re-created ourselves in this misery, this shit of politics, because we do not like who we are, do it now, *bonita*, because we are going to die tomorrow, and she did it. Back in the States, press and television reporters pummeled her with questions about her relationship to Fidel and the Kennedys. There were rumors spurred by Walter Winchell's widely echoed column, "Art, Sex and Treason." She said nothing.

The critics had all agreed: Ruth Cohen's *Cuban Stories* set an impossible standard in the cunning art of artlessness. "After Ms. Cohen," wrote a sacrilegious enthusiast in the *New York Times*, "Walker Evans, heretofore our coolest master of transparency, is revealed to have corroded his subjects with self-referring and self-aggrandizing emotion." The suddenly famous rookie photographer, who would soon develop an overmastering need to become in her life as anonymous as her camera, had worked with an authority of directness that hadn't, of course, actually escaped Evans, but she had seen what Evans had not seen—seen before anyone else who practiced her craft, the emergence of the postmodern body, self-stylized and trapped in perpetual political theater, but somehow shedding the light of unearthly grace, like those suffering, balletic bodies in the crucifixion scenes of Titian and Tintoretto. She had discovered that agony was the mother of beauty. Her photographs were contemporary, and they were old.

But certainly she was more impulsive by far, and still very much the genius of the moment in comparison to this anxious man who comes striding powerfully toward her, whose contact with the moment is only an ideal of his writing, only rarely achieved. She already knows, has always already known, and so she says, "If you wish to see Larry, we'll see Larry. At 8:00, I'll call the clinic." Thank God, Ruth once told Larry privately, there's no Emergency Room within striking distance, or we'd be there once a week.

He replies, "I could call him at home, but it's probably too early. I'll call anyway, I'm calling now. Don't try to stop me."

She checks her watch and says: "Honey, it's 5:47 a.m."

Ruth had stepped into fifty-degree water to the knee; she has no towel; she's been on the platform since 4:00.

Oblivious, and with rising irritation, the paranoid sees the truth beneath the façade: "You think I'm insane? Show me a little concern."

She only says, "Lucky, I'm just a little tired."

"5:47? Good. He'll be home."

Ruth says nothing.

"His two-month-old is no doubt up. They're bottle-feeding this new one and Larry's playing the role of the mother."

She shivers. She says, "Larry plays no roles."

"What are you implying? That I do?"

She says, "I'm cold. Let's go in."

"I don't want to go in. Pay attention to me. Larry's been up every two hours since midnight, sparing his wife, who's been through enough. He'll appreciate the liberation of dealing with an adult. I have to call. Why did he give me the number if he won't face me in an emergency? I need outside help. I'm calling, goddamn it."

Ruth says, "Hug me, I'm cold."

Lucchesi ignores the request (if in fact he's heard it) and says, "I would humiliate myself before a man that I admire and trust if I make the call, is that it? You're implying that I should spare *you*. This is about me, not you."

She says, "Admire and trust? You revere him. You're going to outlive me, Lucky." She doesn't want him to say, "I don't want to outlive you," though she wouldn't mind hearing it just once. He knows that her parents died of heart failure in their mid-fifties, that her episodes of arrhythmia have become more frequent, and long-running, the last one occurring on a grueling, solitary row across the lake. He believes that Larry can fix anything.

He says, "Ruth, there was blood on the toilet paper."

She's watching him, as she so often watches him, with concealed alarm. She says: "How will you manage after I'm dead? You can barely make a sandwich. Lucky, you need to practice living.

Okay. We'll drive down to Utica to see Larry, who'll say, 'In this emergency, I prescribe Preparation H.'"

"I don't appreciate the humor, but I take your point. I can't make the call at this hour. Which is why you have to make the call. Now, if you love me."

"I'll make you breakfast, because I love you."

"You always make me breakfast. What's that got to do with anything?"

He takes her arm and they start for her cabin. She's remembering his joke about how in tennis the meaning of love is well understood, because in tennis when you have love you have nothing.

She shudders again in the chill and her husband, at last noticing, says, "You must be cold."

She's trying not to think, I can't give this man what he needs. This man can't give me what I need. This man may be unreachable.

❈

Sun rise—white fire flaring off the lake as Lucchesi, unpurified by light, swiftly downs two hefty bowls of oatmeal, spiked lavishly with brown sugar and fresh blueberries, because this is a man whose anxieties make no impact on his outrageous appetite. Then to the sink directly he goes, because it calms him to wash dishes—sweep floors and dust, wash clothes and windows, disinfect (daily) the toilet and (weekly) the interior of the refrigerator; it relieves him to square up the several tottering piles of her geological texts. (What is your interest in rocks, Ruth? My interest in rocks, Lucky, is an interest in tranquility.) And now with suppressed violence he dries and puts away the dishes as he gripes to Ruth—who else is there? who better?—about the absence of social and political dimension to his work, while she notes in her mind but must not risk mentioning that it appears to comfort him more than a little to vocalize his mantra of self-flagellation: "Compared to *Cuban Stories*, my work is trivial. I produce triviality because I, myself, am trivial," to which she answers, as always, "No, never," but it makes no difference, because he's on the verge of taking up again the blood-on-the-toilet-paper-theme, when on National Public Radio they're assaulted by another friendly analysis of George W. Bush's UN ultimatum to Saddam Hussein. Ruth is disgusted, with Bush, not her husband, who under her influence has suffered political sea change. He is apoplectic, and almost happy, for the subject he's about to vocalize has been changed from looming cancer of the bowel (his) to the looming cancer of Iraq, the blood on Bush's toilet paper, and suddenly Lucchesi's gone, absorbed into the initial phase of a distended diatribe, another of his morning rites, the content of which Ruth does not find disagreeable, though she'd prefer not to think about the world made by politics. It's the tone, it's the volcanic spewing of the bile, it's the desert that he creates around them when he's fully launched—she'd walk away if only she could do so without causing another, and much worse, kind of outburst. Ruth hates these regular breakfast baths in bitterness. She blames the leaders of nations, mass murderers every one of them, for robbing her of a private life with this man. She feels trapped, but is about to take the chance, about to say, "I can't take this anymore, Lucky, starting out every morning like this, I'm going for a long walk," when she's saved by a knock on the door.

They're stunned. Ruth is afraid. Except for the occasions (more frequent than you'd guess) when one or the other knocked shyly on the other's door, they hadn't ever, when together occupying the same cabin, heard a knock. Not for twelve years. In these parts, people keep to themselves. Not once the irritation of UPS or FedEx. And no mailman either. They drive every ten days to Eagle Bay, eight miles away, for groceries, and to check their post office box, to find it empty except for utility bills. They have no friends or acquaintances in the area, or in any other area. Not excepting Larry, who is neither friend nor acquaintance, but something far greater.

Lucchesi says, "The Raven?" and goes for the door. Ruth says, Wait. She pulls from under the bed the always-loaded double-barreled twelve gauge. Puts it to her shoulder. This place is remote.

❇

Anyone who needed to determine the whereabouts of Ruth Cohen, the scarlet photographer, as she was called in the tabloids of the early sixties, could have learned with strenuous effort that she lived in upstate New York—not in the sophisticated Catskills but in the obscurity of the true upstate, north of Utica, sixty-seven miles exactly north by northeast at Ninth Lake. But until the United States embarked upon its course in Iraq, no one had thought to seek her out, and among those few who remembered her name no one any longer cared (except two) about what she'd done so long ago in Cuba, when the world, she thought, was about to come to an end. Without bothering to revisit the great early work, the critics, in recent years, when they mentioned her at all, uniformly wrote her off with a single sentence: "Hers is the wilted salad of yesterday's avant-garde."

Now, though, on the eve of another international showdown, someone at *The New Yorker* remembered: a geriatric fact checker named Leon Szaflarski, who knew little about photography, who owned a rare, signed copy of the first edition of her first and only book, and who had met her thirty-nine years ago at a reception in her honor at a downtown gallery—because he needed so very much to lay eyes on the controversial artist whose photo did not adorn her book's jacket—and who had, on the spot, fallen fatally in love with her. Believing (with all his heart) that his long-nourished crush afforded him over the years ever keener insight into her political relevance, lonely Leon passed on a note to the editor, along with his copy of the book: "Look at these pictures Lois and think of what Ruth Cohen could do in Iraq. Do you see? Just like Cuba!" And Lois Gint, the barracuda of the cutting edge, saw immediately and set her researchers to the task of determining just how pathetic were the economic circumstances of the fugitive photographer, so that if at all possible she could "ram this assignment so hard up Cohen's ass she'll squeal for more."

This is what they found: That shortly after her Cuban adventure Ruth Cohen was linked ambiguously to violent death in Havana. That she was living with an unsuccessful, though not utterly scorned, novelist, Thomas Lucchesi, whose income was limited to social security earned for a humiliating stint done long ago at an obscure college in the Middle West. That Cohen's small but steady flow of royalties on her breakthrough of 1963 (and its seven reprintings in ten years) were just about, in Lois's rendition, "pissed out." That she refused to do commercial projects, having done so many in the seventies and eighties, and having loathed it all. That between Cohen and Lucchesi it was difficult to imagine how they could sustain themselves without forgoing medical insurance, and so much else.

Lois reads the memos, then quickly displays the genius for which she is known. She takes step #2 in the scheme: Contacts an ex-paramour at the State Department, who back-channels to Baghdad Lois's proposal, together with the relevant details of Cohen's Cuban experience and its scandalous aftermath. When she's wired a week later in the affirmative ("Baghdad enthusiastic but only if Cohen") she assembles her staff: "We're going to massage Saddam's historic sense of himself and Cohen is our masseuse. We're not contacting her by FedEx or even courier. Forget the phone because I have an idea—I'm going to send that smitten fact checker up there. I'll stick her into Baghdad and for $300,000 she'll bring me Saddam's asshole on a platter. Let's get Ruth Cohen, lads, and make *The New Yorker* hotter than the *National Inquirer*. Iraq? Don't make me laugh—I wrack and I ruin."

❊

Lois Gint flies the enamored fact checker to Syracuse ("the kidney stone of America," says Lois) where Leon rents a car. At the rental agency, the cheapest that Lois's assistant could find (on Lois's instruction), where they dispense no maps of New York state, or of any other state, the clerk hands Leon the keys and tells him to drive east on the Thruway to "that hole, Utica." There he can make inquiry at a local gas station. Leon asks, "Can you perhaps just indicate how I'd get from Utica to Old Forge and the North Country, perhaps?" The clerk responds, "In Utica, they call themselves the Gateway to the Adirondacks. Force 'em to live up to their fame. Because how should I know?"

Leon drives to Utica and asks at a gas station, where he's given precise directions to Old Forge but not to Ninth Lake because the attendant, a teenager, has never heard of Ninth Lake, and neither has his father, the station manager, who declares "that particular chain of lakes up north goes up to number eight but I don't believe there is a number nine, unless you're confused by Racquette Lake, or possibly Blue Mountain Lake. My son has put you on the path to Old Forge, but I wouldn't go myself. Neither would my son. Or my ex-wife. Don't hesitate, fella. Go straight to Old Forge and throw yourself on their mercies."

❂

Leon Szaflarski has two problems, the location of so-called Ninth Lake being the lesser of the two. He's a life-long New Yorker. This is his major problem. When he was sixteen, he'd taken a course in Driver's Education, passed the exam and acquired a license, dutifully renewed through the years. Ten years ago, he took a refresher course, in order, as he told a fellow fact checker, "to put some romance in my life." He did not own a car and had no desire to rent one. It was the idea of driving, because in his heart driving is having a golden-thighed girlfriend in the convertible with the top down, summer of '56. Aside from the time spent with an instructor, Leon's never driven. Nor has he ever had a girlfriend.

He found the drive from Syracuse to Utica exciting, he could handle it, though his shirt was damp when he arrived. Good thing the Thruway is a well-maintained superhighway. No oncoming; gentle curves; lanes wide and smooth. Occasionally he allowed himself to look about at the green fields—the lushness, the expanse, the cows and the woodchucks and the rolling terrain and he, Leon, the pastorally deprived, actually doing it at sixty-five miles per hour.

When he presses on due north of Utica on Route 12, he's looking about more than occasionally, because he believes that he's relaxed, but the steady rise in elevation as he leaves the Mohawk Valley has put some steadily rising tension into his neck and shoulders. At the Alder Creek split of Routes 12 and 28, where 28 angles northeast to Old Forge, he sees under the sign for 12 the word that he'd encountered only once before, in a poem by Hart Crane. *Booneville*, that's the word: "There's no place like Booneville though, Buddy... For early trouting... But I kept on the tracks." Abruptly, in the failing light, he pulls over hard, skidding onto the rough shoulder, so much the better to sink into his seizure, transfixed, contemplating the word and experiencing the rush he has known only from reading the master poets of the English language, and from *Cuban Stories*, and from gazing upon Ruth herself, once thirty-nine years ago. Six miles ahead, due north on Route 12, Booneville. It would be like making love to Ruth to go to Booneville.

Potholed 28, a winding two-laner with much oncoming of the

swaying tractor trailer variety—barreling down to obliterate him. Leon needs urgently to pee, but won't risk pulling over in the full dark to the obscure shoulder as stress tension in the neck builds radically—excruciating to glance left or right. Where is the headlights switch? Where is it? He can't hold it much longer. Here in the foothills of the Adirondacks a driving rain with intermittent hail and Leon hasn't eaten since the bagel and coffee at LaGuardia fourteen hours ago—hail now like golf balls, no sleep the night before, the windshield fogging over where is it? The defroster thing? Can't hold it much longer. Where is the windshield wiper lever? Or is it a button on the dash on the wheel on the floor? Tries a button: Heavy Metal at ear splitting levels. Can't turn it off. *The oncoming, better not look on the dash on the wheel on the floor.* He's not holding it.

Old Forge, exhausted beyond description, his good suit, the one he picked out just for Ruth, his entire outfit, even the shoes all soaked through with sweat and urine. Finds a motel and sleeps like a dead man.

No place like Booneville though, Buddy.

❂

Leon awakens in late morning to find the weather cleared, the mountains visible and close, and his body in pain from the deep, thoroughgoing wrack of yesterday's adventure, as he shuffles stiff and bent about the room, contemplating his insulted pinstripe suit: totally wrinkled and odiferous. Thinking he'll need to make inquiries about Ninth Lake, because with his luck he'll be driving in the dark again on a wild goose chase. Shaving now at noon and wanting to correct the Manhattan pallor of the homely face in the mirror, starved for a fresh face even at his age. Leon believes that a suntan would improve his face. Leon says to the mirror, "At least my shoulder bag is good looking": by Kenneth Cole, black and expensive, the rare luxury of a narrow life. *Jeez, I wish I were a good looking guy, I'll take a day off and get a tan because in Old Forge they won't have same day dry cleaning service.* Just for a day, just for tomorrow, he wants to be handsome: to transform a face (*for Ruth*) that not even the most fiendish of plastic surgeons could correct, it was so bland.

In Old Forge there is in fact a same day service dry cleaners, located across from the Big Moose Diner, a short walk from the motel, where the clerk recommends the Big Moose because the locals who hang out there maybe can answer his question about Ninth Lake which he'd never heard of, "which doesn't mean much since I'm a newcomer to this eye sore. I should have stayed in Utica."

They tell him at the cleaners that he can have his suit in an hour, but he's already made up his mind to spend the day sunning himself by the drained pool back at the motel, its dry concrete caked with dead leaves, and he there alone, imagining a journey to a world elsewhere. He has the vision; he wants the experience.

They tell him at the diner, they're curiously eager to tell him, that on a detailed map of the region he might notice a tiny lake, unnumbered and unnamed, between 8th and Racquette, owned for much of the last century by a minor Rockefeller and his descendants, all of them undistinguished ("this is why we summer in the low rent Adirondacks") and possessed by a need for privacy and even oblivion that extended to their property. It was this branch of Rockefellers that could, without a license or a license plate, drive with impunity, that never registered with the Social Security Administration, whose greasy longhaired male members during the Vietnam era did not register for the draft, and got away with it, that had made a gigantic political contribution to ensure that the brutally rutted lane (you could not call it a road) leading for a mile off 28 to the lake, would never be paved or widened or marked in any way, so decreed by special and unanimous agreement of both houses of the state legislature, signed by Governor Nelson A. Rockefeller, and furthermore by said decree stipulated that said lake would never be named or numbered, unto perpetuity. Upon the death of John D. Rockefeller VII, the summer house was demolished, the foundation dug up and carted away, and the lot deeded over to one Ruth Cohen, because her book, *Cuban Stories*, had afforded John D. "more pleasure" (so stated his will, publicly read at Town Hall in Eagle Bay) "than my wife ever did in her passional prime."

They said, "Now you want to know how it got to be called Ninth Lake, and we're dying to tell you. Twelve years ago, when Cohen and her consort came up here and built those cabins (we've never seen them), the Poet Laureate of Eagle Bay named her The Lady of Ninth Lake, and it stuck. She heard about what the Poet Laureate had done because up here your business is known, and she took a shine to it and insisted that the post office up in Eagle Bay change her box number to Ninth Lake, we don't know how she got her way, it is an outrage, and that's how the mail is addressed, though we don't know who would write to such hermits, nobody's been on their property that we know of. You might be the first. We're low on stories around here. If you get it, friend, bring us the story, bring it fast."

Leon asks, "It's not down in any map?"

They reply, "True places never are."

❃

Is it possible to experience the awesome impact of one's own charisma? A metaphysical nicety entertained by the mind of Leon Szaflarski, though he was sure that he'd never had any charisma until this moment of the dangerous turn, as he shoots the gap of the oncoming, crossing the highway half way up a steep grade— onto the rutted lane off 28. *Ruth's road*. He knew that he was different this morning, that he was radiating the invisible reality of power. The harrowing drive to Old Forge had transformed him, literally overnight, into a composed veteran of the highway, a one-handed driver, who feels himself afloat in a rare state of self-approval, in command of so many nameless things. He likes his complexion, the crisply pressed suit that he'd always worn so well, the burnished glow of his oxfords. Believes that she'll sense his newfound psychological force. That she'll kind of like him, you know, in a way, which is all that he hopes for.

Inside the Kenneth Cole (because an invitation might be extended, it's not out of the question) a change of socks but no change of underwear (because he wears no underwear); a case containing his toiletries; his signed copy of *Cuban Stories* ("To Leo") and Lucchesi's long out-of-print first novel, *The Prostate Dialogues*, purchased for twice the cover price at the Gotham Book

Mart ("Wise Men Fish Here"), a book in the difficult experimental style that had won its author a handful of academic admirers specializing in Hyper-Postmodernism. And two letters, one for Ruth, the other, deviously, for Lucchesi. Handwritten by Lois Gint. The unrefusable offers.

The lane ends in a sparsely graveled cul de sac. Parked there, a white mud-spattered, '92 Jeep Wrangler. Leon smoothes his hair in the rear view mirror, then again in the window after he slams shut his door. Straightens his tie and then starts down the embankment through the, what do you call them? Christmas trees? Does not see the cabins until he emerges into the clearing, and then he sees them from the rear, woodpile and wheelbarrow, and some kind of thing out there on the water, like a stage or something. Knocks on the door of cabin #1. No answer. Approaches cabin #2. The tie. The hair. It's 8:27. A voice from within, male, harsh, saying Fuck Bush. This is the place. Knocks. Radio off. All quiet. Knocks again. *Shouldn't have done that. They heard it the first time.* The door swings open and he's paralyzed, only in part by the shotgun aimed at his head. Because he's not so scared that he can't take in the great legs. He's found her—who is trying hard not to imagine his bloody blasted body, who is trying to make a decision about a bespectacled stranger standing in the sun, like a forlorn cherub *what they always look like* last seen in the company of children when a child himself, saying Ruth, Ruth *how does he know my name?* I'm just Leon *and you let them into your house because they are bland* Lois Gint sent me with offers *because their cars are broken down and they need to make a call and can they have a glass of water* I was born in the Bronx on Belmont

Ave *then you let them in no sign of forcible entry* Lois Gint, The New Yorker *and they shoot you blandly* They're in the bag, the letters, you know the Bronx? Dion and The Belmonts, where Republicans fear to tread, the Bronx, Smile a little, say something, I'm scared *they rape blandly with forcible entry* Two letters, one for each, in the bag next to my toiletries and a pair of socks and two books, I have given you the complete inventory *because I let him in who looks so pathetic if he tries to go into that bag* I'm slowly dropping my bag, I'm taking off my jacket, I'm stepping back slowly from the bag, The bag is innocent *then he sets this house on fire* I can't drop my pants *pervert* I could but I shouldn't, Don't make me do that *I should kill this*—I am Leon Szaflarski, remember? I am Polish, I am not a Polack! Laugh a little—*kill this bland and pudgy bastard* I detect a smile, We are all three now smiling together, I am Leon, I am your friend Leon.

She lowers the shotgun.

Leon says, "I've never been in a cabin."

❁

Dear Lucchesi,

You are not now, nor will you ever be, a star. Hence, we at *The New Yorker* do not wish to fuck you. You have long understood this, and you seethe, even as you abominate all that I stand for. Read on, because I'm going to make you happy, you hypocrite.

We are aware of Michel Foucault's mysterious admiration for your "writing," it makes you proud, but we are not impressed, because we have read you—here, at *The New Yorker*, we read everything, including the tedious experimental edge of so-called "literary fiction." (You believe the phrase is, or should be, a redundancy; I believe the phrase is, or should be, a contradiction in terms.) Were you by some corruption of commerce to become in your dotage a star, we would not care to publish you, we think so little of you, but do not despair, seethe no more: I'm going to thrill you.

Accordingly, I hereby set my standards aside and offer to publish a work of yours of whatever genre (it concerns me not), not to exceed 2500 words, for a fee of $7,500, said work to appear in *The New Yorker* not later than three months from the date of this missive. In addition, we will print a full-page, thoroughly airbrushed photo of you by Richard Avedon, who we'll transport to your woodland hideaway. Richard will scream, but you will be given choice of photo. The glamorous author pic disgusts you, of course, but with the exception of that cockteaser Pynchon, who imagines that millions desire to gaze upon his image, all of you "artists" lust for it. We also agree to run a 250-word side bar, a fawning bio-bibliographical essay to be signed by my fiction editor, but written by you. All of your expenses to, in, and from Baghdad to be absorbed by the Kotex of my expense account. Yes, *Baghdad*. I need you because I need Cohen for *Baghdad*. Consult Cohen. Should all go well with Saddam, upon your return I agree to reprint your three hopelessly out of print "fictions" in my new Knopf series, "Post-Contemporary Probings for the Literate and the Beautiful." A $25,000 advance and Sonny's usual royalty structure (2% on the first 100,000 copies sold, 5% thereafter) is understood.

This letter and its duplicate (enclosed) constitutes a contract binding all parties, individual and institutional, named and/or alluded to herein, after you sign and date both copies and return one to me. You have one week from receipt of this letter to get a signed and dated copy to me, or no deal. Seven days, Lucchesi.

Here's the rub. Should Cohen not agree to *Baghdad*, this offer, which gives me vaginitis even as I write, is in the crapper.

Yours,

✺

Dear Cohen,

How do I love thee? Let me count the ways: Fidel, JFK, Saddam Saddam Saddam.

I've arranged for you to see the man, in Baghdad. They'll take you to one of his forty-seven Presidential Palaces, where you'll meet one of his fifty-seven doubles. You will shoot the double, and then—satisfied that your camera is not piercing his double's body with septicemic light rays—the real Saddam steps forward and says, I am Saddam Hussein himself, I am Saddam. You agree to give the photos exclusively to *The New Yorker*. $300,000 plus expenses. We pay the taxes.

You wonder, since I can have my pick of photographers, why you, a has-been? Because Saddam agrees to you and nobody else but you. Do you for a moment believe that we captains of the media haven't tried before? You touch something in the man's sense of history, what he famously calls repetition with a difference. He is the difference, the man who believes that he will make us at long last eat it. Think, as he does, of the shimmering parallels. Cuba and the U.S. Iraq and the U.S. Weapons of mass destruction poised to devastate the homeland, ours and his. Fidel and JFK; Saddam and Bush, and you the magical link, the lubricated female. In his vision of pan-Arab apocalypse, Saddam is the Fidel who succeeds, Bush the JFK who fails. He, Saddam Hussein, hands another Bush a failed presidency.

We have of course informed him of what was widely rumored in the period of your big splash: that you made the beast with two backs with Fidel and, upon your return, at a party at Bobby Kennedy's, with JFK himself. You had extreme good looks, back then at any rate. We sent a copy of *Cuban Stories* to the man along with copies of the relevant Winchell columns and a copy of Gore Vidal's recent *The Camelot Diaries*, in which the story of your romp with Jack is so wittily told. Gore was there. Gore *knows*. Even when Gore's not there, Gore knows. Saddam will sit for you and you alone. (You have me over a barrel.) Through you Saddam becomes part of the magnetic homoerotic chain—Fidel, JFK, himself, all plunging the same hole, and he the final plunger, the Arab stud supreme. You have a thing for men of power and Saddam is the ultimate aphrodisiac. (What possibly can Lucchesi do for you? I am at a loss to understand.) You are not *required*, of course, to fuck Saddam. He's not bad looking, as Arabs go, especially when he doesn't rag his head. Do as you wish. Saddam does as Saddam does.

Along with your photos we will run a tastefully suggestive side bar on your relations with great men, including Saddam—so you might as well indulge your proclivities. Saddam does not insist (on the side bar); I insist.

Your will is Lucchesi's, if you love. But your will and his belong to me, because I am the devouring lover who intends to consume you both in the pages of *The New Yorker*. You are bitter, alienated, stymied, and full of loathing for America. I'm going to take you inside. I am the cure.

I advise you to read the enclosure now carefully before you read another word of this. It is my offer to your husband.

Long ago you abandoned commercial work, because you are above it, but can you possibly deny the man you love the notice that the two of you believe, against all evidence, he deserves? The true lover sacrifices self to the needs of the beloved. The true lover relinquishes. Do you truly love, Ms. Cohen? Lucchesi trusts that you do, and so do I.

You have nine days from receipt of this letter, or no deal. Note that Lucchesi has seven. Pointless to agonize, darling—in two weeks you're leaving for *Baghdad*. Because I have you over a barrel.

Yours,

The three stand apart in cold sunshine. A man reading, turning his back to the others as he reads. This man is thrilled and humiliated. A woman, also reading, with a loaded shotgun at her feet, the barrel pointed in the direction of the third party, the stranger. Her face registers total defeat. And the child-like man, the stranger, gazing with entrapped attention, amazed and flooded with joy to be so close to the woman again, but his joy shadowed already by its imminent departure, his joy departing even as it is felt. Would he be invited in? Might this be the beginning of something? It was ludicrous to think certain thoughts, but how can he keep himself from thinking certain thoughts? Perhaps she would offer hot chocolate and homemade cinnamon rolls on this chilly morning, in the cabin before the roaring fireplace, Leon and Ruth, toasting each other with cups of hot chocolate as she agrees to have actual correspondence with him in the final phase of his life, *Your friend, Ruth, Affectionately, Leon*, if only she would, the final phase would be nicer than all the other phases, including his so-called youth phase. *I'm so close to her now who I can't touch, if I could hug her just once, I hope I'll touch her hand before I leave*, thinks the child-like man injured for decades by desire that a child cannot know: *Dear Ruth, Dear Leon*.

The glowering Lucchesi holds up his letter and says to Ruth, "We're going to have to—"

Ruth interrupts, holding up hers, "I know. She was kind enough to include a copy of yours with mine."

Lucchesi would like to grill her, here and now, on what he will later call "your obvious prior relationship," "your involvement" with Leon Szaflarski, but he restrains himself, he'll save it for later, when they're alone. In the meanwhile, he'll brood and feed his instinct for resentment and the self-isolation which he once judged for Ruth, in a lucid and contented moment, as "my genius for masochism," to which Ruth had replied, "You have a taste for suffering, Lucky, especially your own."

Lucchesi turns on Leon, "Is there anything else? If not, goodbye."

Leon says, "Actually. No, nothing more, not really. But if you don't mind, I'm sorry, I wonder if Ms. Cohen, if you would kindly Ms. Cohen re-sign my copy of *Cuban Stories*? I brought it in my bag. See, you wrote here, 'To Leo.' If you could just write 'To Leon,' or just squeeze in a little 'n' here, just put the little 'n' in, would you do that? I suppose I could put the 'n' in myself, who would know the difference except me and of course you, though it would be nicer if you—I'm going."

Lucchesi says, "Goodbye."

Ruth says, "Wait. If you have a pen."

Leon says, "Oh, yes."

He hands her the pen. As she takes it, her fingers brush his. She signs the book, then hands it to him with a faint smile.

Leon says, "Thank you."

She says, "Do I know you?"

"In a manner of speaking."

Lucchesi says, "What do you mean by know?"

"We met at a signing party for *Cuban Stories*. I said, Hello, I admire your work. You said, Thank you for saying so. That was all. Many years ago. We were younger then… We were young. You still, of course… you look… I'm sorry."

Ruth says, "Thank you. Thank you for saying so. Nice to have met you... again. Good luck, Leon."

She offers her hand. They shake.

Leon looks down at his hand. Then he looks at Ruth and says, "Thank you, Ms. Cohen. If I don't see you again, good luck to you, and to you too, Mr. Lucchesi. I brought a nice copy of *The Prostate Dialogues*. Mint condition, really. Maybe you—"

Lucchesi cuts him off with a stare.

Leon leaves—stealing glances at his hand.

❋

The double-barreled twelve gauge lies between them still. ("A gun," he'd said on the day she bought it, "once introduced into the narrative, eventually becomes the agent of the central action and must fulfill its destiny—tragic or farcical, we never know in advance.")

She hands him the letter. He reads. She watches the man, whose surname she's already forgotten, fade away between the cabins and up the embankment, into the trees. With elaborate, tight-lipped care, Lucchesi folds and replaces the letter in the envelope. Then as if on cue, in one furious motion she picks up the shotgun, puts it hard to her shoulder, whirls shoreward and fires both barrels simultaneously, out over the water. The massive recoil kicks her on her ass.

"Farce," he says, without mirth. "Pure farce."

Her tears are bitter.

He offers a hand.

She pushes it away—hard.

She says, "Put your backpack in order."

"In this crisis we hike?"

"No. Climb."

"Please. Take my hand."

"I like it down here."

He sits beside her.

He says, "Ruth."

No response.

He touches her thigh.

She takes no notice.

"Remember," she says, "Whiteoak Canyon? We're going to drive to the bottom of Whiteoak Canyon and climb to the top."

"We're old, Ruth. Me worse than you."

"When we reach the Fire Road running along the rim, we'll be totally depleted, mentally as well as physically, by the treacherous grade of the final ascent. At the Fire Road, we're tempted to go back."

"We do not go back. Obviously."

"No. We hang a left on the Fire Road. A half-mile more to the base of the rock tower that looms over Rift Valley. When we reach the Tower, exhilarated and exhausted, we insist on scaling the rock-fastened ladder of iron rungs. We insist. Straight up the final thirty yards to the Tower summit."

"I would not insist."

"Straight up we go, Thomas."

"Try not to use the collective pronoun."

"At the summit, we rehydrate and tear into the sandwiches

and the fruit, recklessly conserving nothing, not even a saltine, for the long haul back. The view of Blue Mountain Lake—do you remember that view?"

"I choose not to remember."

"On the north face of the Tower we scale backwards, down another iron ladder, badly rusted. Will it hold? We give it not a thought."

"The pronoun, Ruth."

"At the bottom, the ill-named Big Woods Trail, which traverses a steep and densely bouldered field of jumbled granite. Irregular, sharp-edged, dew-slippery. Do you remember the cruel field of granite?"

"I remember your blood on the rocks."

"The Fire Road again—back to the Canyon mouth. We cannot possibly take another step. Down the Canyon. We are destroyed. Down the Canyon. We want to curl up with our mother, our hard and breastless mother of the rocks, and sleep forever a dreamless sleep."

"Not me."

"Our voices in all that silence scare us. Fast, down the Canyon, gravity our mortal enemy now, but we no longer care. Fast, like barn-sour horses, possessed by desire to return home—but no home to return to—stumbling over exposed gigantic tree roots, our rock mother refuses to let them in, falling many times, sustaining cuts and abrasions and injuries whose extent we'll not be aware of until the next day. If we leave within the hour, we're back to the jeep by 7:00, 7:30."

He caresses her thigh.

"At my age," he says. "At my age." Pauses. "With your heart." Pauses. "Ruth, it will be totally dark by 5:30."

"The last hour through the lower reaches of the Canyon is precipitous, but so what. We skinny-dip in moonlight, in the deep cold pool behind the last of the Canyon's nine Falls—we cavort among America's last native Brookies, in fifty-two degree water. Do you remember when we skinny-dipped? Do you remember what we did—after we skinny dipped?"

"On a multi-colored beach towel. On a great slab of granite. With vigor."

"We at last emerge from the Canyon without hospitalizing damage. Or we don't emerge, because we can't emerge, as we huddle in the advancing chill, fog-shrouded, awaiting the dawn and another hiker who will attempt to summon a medical evacuation team on his cell phone, which cannot function deep inside our granite tomb."

A considerable pause.

He takes his hand from her thigh.

"Very nice. Yes. A plan for double suicide. And you render it all with such lyric relish. A final tomb scene. *Aida*. *Liebestod*. How romantic, in a nineteenth-century, German sort of way. The only proper answer to Lois Gint, or so you believe. But I don't want to die. With or without love, I don't want to die. What does Ruth want?"

"I want you to make eight sandwiches. Not all of them peanut butter and jelly, as is your wont. Don't forget the Bing cherries, the saltines, the dried mango slices, or the marinated artichoke hearts. Pack the protein bars, as many as possible. Do not forget the protein bars or the sun-dried tomatoes. Never mind the saltines. Forget the saltines."

He laughs.

She says, "You think I'm funny?"

"How is it possible that a woman in apparent blackest despair can manage to sustain such avid interest in food?"

"One does what one can to keep the end from being hard."

"Forget the saltines?" He pauses, cunningly, feeling a little wicked. He says, "How about the Animal Crackers?"

The Geology of God

He believes that jokes defer our awareness of death. (I don't seek to defer.) Fossils, he said, when first he learned of my geological interests, are only animal crackers of exceptional anatomical detail. And exceptional beauty, I replied, but beauty fashioned by no human artist, telling no human story. My animal crackers please children, he says, they're delicious! (Yes, he buys animal crackers.) Fossils, I reply, are sustenance for an undernourished composure (mine)—deep-reaching sedation for the mind (mine) disgusted with this spectacle of corruption and slaughter that you call history, that so fascinates you. Fossils are cold. (His joke is lame.)

He talks to me about the flowers, ferns, lichens and mosses of the Adirondacks. Partridgeberry, sheep laurel, trout lilies, fiddlehead ferns, crustose lichen and caribou moss. The names of things are lies. There are no caribou in the Adirondacks. Never were. The earth is 4.6 billion years old. Where were they all then, the partridgeberry, the sheep laurel, the fiddlehead ferns? He calls the

Adirondacks his cozy companions. Look, he says, upside down ice cream cones! Nippletops! I tell him your nippletops give no suck and what you call nature is but the thinnest veneer of the earth. Your ecological concern is poignant, Thomas, and pointless. In time, he says, the Rockies may crumble? No, I say. Not may, *will*. Wind and rain, grain by grain by grain, and all shall be well again. Gibraltar tumbles, he says, but our love is here to stay. No, I tell him. Our love cannot stay, because even were we immortal there'd be no *here* for love to stay *on*. I've found in geological time the equalizer to fend off the bitter morning litanies of his political bile. To which I now reply: "The distribution of the world's deserts is only temporary." I can tell, he says, that you find the idea amusing. You like the phrasing too much. Mordant Ruth, he says. Yes, I say. Now suck on this: The earth is 4.6 billion years old. Has no bearing, he says. Totally incomprehensible. You can't scare me with your geological time. Think, I say, of those 4.6 billion years as if they were all compressed into a single year. Good, he says. That's good. We make analogies to console and enlighten ourselves—metaphor-making is the chief glory of human consciousness. (He's so clearly a writer.) It all begins, Thomas, on January 1. The dinosaurs don't appear until December 1. They're extinct by December 26. Humans appear about 8 p.m. on December 31. The average life span of a privileged Westerner in the early twenty-first century is a half-second of geological time. The half-second before midnight. He says, Why does it delight you to tell me that? Go ahead, I say, make a joke about your half-second. The delight you take, he says, in the news of geological time is more terrifying than the news itself, but I don't give a damn about geological time. It's the time of Ruth that I care for. I tell him it soothes me to think of myself as too trivial a part of the geological process even for the word trivial or infinitesimal to do justice to my insignificance. The thought of complete obliteration in, and by, the process, is a blessing. He said, You have re-discovered the Desert Fathers, you've found God in geological time. Humanity is trivial? Yes, I say, and all of its works. You scorn what I cherish as nature? Yes. Your pleasure, Ruth, in rocks, is morbid. Yes. Morbid is the point. All of written history fits into the last forty-two seconds of the year. How do you like the analogical mind now, Mr. L? Feel enlightened and consoled?

Unlike his, my animal crackers have been cold a long, long time, but they, also, are delicious.

He wants to go to Baghdad—cares too much for me to admit it, but this is what he wants.

❂

She's driving to Whiteoak Canyon because she always drives, not because he can't, but because he won't. Ruth, any more ice cream in the fridge? I wonder if there are any more Klondike bars in the fridge? A child-like male at seventy-one. Were she asked, she would say, Enough to say male—and he would agree.

He says, "This old jeep has seen its days, along with my prostate, my colon, et cetera. Sane people would have no trouble swallowing the rage and humiliation. And let us not neglect to mention your deteriorating arrhythmia. You may be on the brink. $300,000, Ruth. You need that defibrillator we can't afford."

She does not respond.

"Say something, Ruth. We've got problems. We've got letters to write."

Nothing.

He says, "I need to point out that my palpitations have taken a turn for the worse."

"A classic symptom of female hysteria."

"Our major appliances are on the brink. We don't travel, we don't go out to dinner. When was the last time we ate out? Talk to me, Ruth."

"Sane people would swallow the rage and humiliation."

"That dying one-hundred-foot hemlock leaning over our cabins is a knife through warm butter and who can afford to have it taken down?"

"It's not dying. Who says that we must answer Lois Gint?"

"Why give her the satisfaction? Is this your point? Let's refuse the money, the publicity, the big boost to our corpsed careers—turn down the opportunity to enter history together, in Baghdad. Let's go on as we always have—alive and not so well in no man's land. Why not? How much longer can we have left, anyway? We don't respond to her letters."

"Or maybe we do respond. Maybe we say, We accept your kind offer."

"When the world teetered over the nuclear abyss forty years ago, you were the intrepid American beauty in Havana. I wasn't there. Lois Gint is dead on about the parallel. Cuba and Iraq. History is a nightmare from which you do not awake. We—you—must under no circumstances go to Baghdad. You especially. Over my dead body."

"Please don't do that with your hand."

"Let me into the nightmare."

"Don't do that when I'm driving."

"What am I doing? JFK."

"What?"

"JFK."

"I'm driving. Stop."

"JFK. How do I rank with King Arthur?"

"You want to do something? I'll pull over and we'll do something."

He takes his hand away.

He says, "In this vehicle the back seat is impossible and up front we have the problem of the stick. Let's save the main event for the Canyon, where we can replay our hot honeymoon hike."

She touches his crotch.

She says, "Don't you want to give me this now?"

"Let's wait—anticipation is good."

"The stick is not a problem," she says, "it's an opportunity."

"Back then, who didn't read those Winchell columns? I remember that knock out photo of you circulating intensely in the aftermath of Dallas. A tragic beauty, Jackie's rival, et cetera. Did Dallas break your heart, Ruth? Time to reveal all. Is it the case, as Lois Gint claims, that you attended a party at Bobby Kennedy's?"

"7:00 pm on the unseasonably warm evening of October 22, 1963."

"You remember exactly?"

"Wouldn't you, if you were twenty-two, and had met the man himself?"

"I'm not a woman—I wasn't there."

"Why've you waited all this time to ask?"

Pause.

"Fear."

"Of what?"

Pause.

"Of what you'd tell me."

"Now you're not afraid?"

"You just missed the turnoff for Route 8."

"There's another way to get there."

Pause.

"I thought that I was the man himself."

"You are."

"If JFK is the man himself, how can I be the man himself?"

"You are the man, Lucky, you are the *man*."

"Tell me the story."

The jeep heads north as the overcast thickens, the morning darkens and a fine mist smears the windshield. Only the wiper on the driver's side functions. He's gazing out at the fog-obscured mountainside to his right, looking in mid-September for painted trillium—a bloom, he well knows, of earliest Spring. For the entire story, he will gaze right, always right, away from Ruth.

"I received a call from a man who said, Hold for Mrs. Kennedy, please. Then a woman says, Hi, this is Ethel Kennedy. I stifled a laugh—I'd been getting crank calls ever since the book appeared. She told me she was an admirer of *Cuban Stories* and would like to invite me to a barbeque at her home. I told her that large gatherings scare me—she assured me that this one would be small, very informal. Strictly family, except for the ambassador to the United Nations, Adlai Stevenson, who always wears suits, he can't help it she said, he'd put her on to my work—the book of the year, she said. Bobby and the kids. And Jackie and the President will try to make it. Jack's two kids and my eight. The kids will take our minds off ourselves. 'I have another one in the oven'—an exact quote. Unless I'd prefer a hotel, they would put me up at their house. Airline tickets would be arranged. My kids like guests, especially young pretty ones. You'll be a big hit. Her voice was so easy to trust."

"Tell it step by step. Give me your impressions of the three-story, white colonial brick mansion with the black shutters, on the sprawling Hickory Hill estate. The three dogs, the ponies, the towering oaks. After Bobby's death, we all bought the coffee table book, *RFK: Hearth and Home*. The two golden Labs, and Tess, the Irish Setter. What was it really like, Ruth? The eleven parakeets."

"It became clear to me early in the evening that Ethel had forgotten to tell anyone but Adlai, who wanted to meet me, that I would be there."

"The kids go crazy for young pretty surprises, like you. As did JFK."

"Jackie knew who I was. She owned the book and asked me if she could send a copy to be signed. The President and Bobby did subtle double-takes. They knew me too, I believed, but not as followers of the recent art photography scene."

"And now we know why. The CIA plots to kill Castro. Were they rogue ventures, or were they approved at the highest levels? Including a plot that involved exploding or poisonous cigars, I can't remember which. Definitely cigars. We know this now. Christ, Ruth. When the chauffeur brought you to the magnificent home in McLean, Virginia were JFK and Jackie already there?"

"I was delivered at 6:30, a half hour early on Ethel's instructions, it turned out. She came to the door. Shorts, tube top, ruddy and athletic. Not at all pregnant looking. She wanted to talk about the book before things got hectic, but had preparations to complete in the kitchen and could use a hand."

"No caterers? No servants? Not realistic."

"None in sight. Then the Attorney General comes into the kitchen while we're making the hamburger patties, looking like her slightly older brother, and in similar attire."

"He wore a tube top?"

"The resemblance was stunning. A spot of shaving cream on his ear. Two tiny cuts on his chin, which he was dabbing with a tissue. Bobby wasn't wearing a tube top."

"What were you wearing?"

"More or less what Ethel was wearing."

"A little less? A little tighter? Hence, Bobby's double take? It wasn't the CIA plot. It was your legs."

"Stevenson is brought into the kitchen by the oldest kid. He's dressed formally, with a red carnation. Grandfatherly, courtly, lecherous. There are shouts from outside, like a gang of kids cheering a touchdown. Bobby, who's putting the finishing touches on the potato salad, says, Uncle Jack. Adlai says, I'll make myself another martini. We file into the living room, which is a minefield of toys, and in comes Jackie, Caroline and John junior. Jackie doesn't look well. Pale, too thin. From where I stand I can see him struggling to emerge from the long black limo, assisted out by a Secret Service agent. He has great difficulty straightening up. Another agent gives him his crutches and the President, as the kids swarm him, comes up the walk, through the door and into the foyer. Dark slacks, a white short sleeved golf shirt. Deeply tanned. In order to get into the living room he must ascend three steps. He hands the agent the crutches and takes the steps sideways. We approach. He's swollen around the eyes, as if he hadn't slept for two days, or were in great pain, or had been weeping for the last thirty minutes. All of which is in absurd contrast to the sudden flash of his smile, the smile of the century, as the kids continue to swarm him. His first words are to the Attorney General. Bobby, he says, I trust you have a coroner on call? Bobby roars. The tan from this distance is somehow a little off."

"Now we know why. The jaundiced reaction to his 10,000 medications. The Addison's disease. Did he flash you the smile of the century as he did his double take when he heard your name? All of this domestic detail is nice, Ruth, but neither of us appreciates the novel of domestic realism. This is a story of politics and passion. Kindly cut to the chase. Give us the epiphany—give us the luminous image."

"How many people remember that they lost a baby in late August of '63? Less than two months before the barbeque."

"A virile, handsome man and a beautiful, fecund mother. In the White House. The nation was never happier, or hornier."

"A son, Patrick he was named. Patrick Bouvier, who lasted two days. They show her her baby. He's held before her by the obstetrician. The image is indelible. Patrick, a blood-smeared newborn—

placed briefly, and bloody, on her breasts and then taken away, forever. Three months later in Dallas, her husband's exploded head lies in her lap, her clothes are blood-soaked, she's crawling after brain fragments on the trunk of the presidential limousine. These are the images she will carry into the closing hours of her life. Domestic details, Thomas. Blood and passion and politics."

"Did you talk to him and what did he say? This is what we want to know. Did a Secret Service agent contact you the next day and invite you to see the President privately the following week, when Jackie would be medicating her grief on the Riviera?"

"When he supposed they were sharing a private moment, I saw Bobby stroke Ethel's abdomen. I saw Jackie wince when she saw what I saw."

"Luminous, but only personal. Did you talk to him, and what did he say?"

"We were eating outside, poolside. The kids had made an ungodly mess, but no one cared. Food everywhere but on their plates. On Adlai's pants. In the pool. Matthew Kennedy is eating Adlai's carnation. The President drags his chair alongside mine. It takes him a while to sit. He says, with great deliberateness, I have not yet looked into your book, which rests these days on Jackie's bedside table, but as you might imagine I know something of the circumstances of those pictures. You were used, Miss Cohen, by men who worked for your country. Your life didn't mean a damn to them. He pauses—I'm tongue-tied. He says, It's easier than you might think for a President of the United States to say, I take full responsibility, I'm sorry. Even to say it on national television, as I did after the Bay of Pigs. And then he is applauded for his courage. His maturity, and so forth. But the lives he puts in harm's way, or ruins, or destroys by his decisions, or indecisions, are wholly abstract. Truman slept the night he ordered the destruction of Hiroshima. You believe Truman was callous? Inhuman? He was presidential. For what you endured, Miss Cohen, I'm sorry. I managed to get out, Thank you, Mr. President. He says, And you did endure—much more than most of us could ever bear."

"Who could resist such a line? He told you that you were a Profile in Courage."

"It was Adlai who made the pass."

"Because a man with the President's physical woes could not do all the womanizing that the negative mythmakers say he did. We know this now. A little here and there, but not that much. A twelve-hour day, seven days a week in the Oval office and all that pain. The myths are absurd. A little here and there, of course."

"At this point his two-year-old son waddles over and says, Daddy, Daddy, pick up John John up. The President reaches over and tousles his hair and the child says, Bo! (which I took to mean no). Pick up John John up, now! The President turns to me and says, Miss Cohen, would you mind lifting my son into my lap? I pick up John junior and as I do he smears my top with ketchup. As I settle him into the President's lap, he smears the President's white shirt, and somehow I lose my balance, and fall forward a little—my face brushed his."

"How could you not lose your balance in such proximity to charisma central?"

"He looked at the red stain on his shirt, and then at mine, and said, The literary types would call this a symbolic moment, but I am not particularly literary, Miss Cohen. Let's not tell Gore Vidal."

"And that was the extent of your contact. And it was Adlai the high-minded, the embittered Eugene McCarthy of his time, who saw this little moment, who you gave the cold shoulder to, and who called Winchell that very night. Adlai the randy liberal, whose feelings of jealousy toward JFK were well-known."

"My surmise exactly. Two days later an item appeared in Winchell's nationally syndicated column."

"Quick, tell me more."

"Something he said in response to Stevenson who had said that U.S. diplomats were the great hope, as the Cuban Crisis had demonstrated. The President laughed in a very hollow way and replied, I look over at State and see a lot of your friends who don't seem to have *cojones*, Adlai, whereas over at Defense it looks as if that's all they've got. They haven't any brains at Defense. This macho crap I read about how we stared down the Russians. We were all scared and we got lucky. At the end, at the door, as we said our goodbyes, Jackie told me that she was having a dinner for some writers and artists and would be honored if I'd come. Sometime between Thanksgiving and Christmas. He chimed in, By then I'll have spent time with your notorious book. John John insists that you be there. Bobby and Ethel put me up in a guest bedroom with a king size bed. Bobby said, Our guests all have good bedfellows. Then he blushed. That night I shared my bed with two of the kids and one of the labs. Both of those kids are dead."

The misting rain has become a steady downpour—the mountains are obscured. Lucchesi sees a sign for Whiteoak Canyon, a quarter mile. The alternate route, a right turn, but Ruth keeps plugging north.

"Didn't you see the sign? Better turn back."

"We're obviously not hiking today, Thomas."

"Where are we going?"

"About twenty minutes more there's an unpaved road that'll take us west about two miles, where we cross over a stream. We park and follow the stream south about two hundred yards, to a place that's dry and secluded beside the stream, beneath a large granite outcrop. Where we have our picnic—and our discussion."

❈

She halts a moment in the wind and points ahead about twenty-five yards. "There," she says. He sees it—thrust up and arcing out over the stream. The great granite outcrop. In shadow, at its base, the protected place they seek.

The man is sitting in the lotus position and waving his rifle and saying, "Come in out of the weather, folks." A slight man of indistinct age, in hunter's camouflage. His face is soft and cheerful. He wears a hearing aid. A beagle lies by, wagging its tail, moaning and crawling toward them on its belly. They come in under the shadow of the rock.

The man says, "Welcome to paradise. Got any food on you?"

Lucchesi replies, "Well, as a matter of—"

The man points his rifle at Lucchesi and says, "Shut your face, dumbo."

A terrible silence.

The man says, "Aw, for Christ sakes, lighten up folks. I was only joshing. We all could use a little joshing once in a while, don't you think? Let's have a proper picnic."

Too late to run.

Ruth says, "May I offer you a sandwich?"

The man points the rifle at her and says, "You just changed the subject on me, lady. Think I wouldn't notice? Now I'm asking you in a nice way, Could you, or could you not, use a little joshing?"

Ruth says, "Yes."

Lucchesi says, "Yes."

The man says, "Was I talking to you, bub?"

In the backpack, a knife with a five-inch retractable blade. Double-edged, savagely serrated on one side. Lucchesi imagines handing the man a sandwich: As the man takes his first bite, he drives it with all his might to the hilt, into the throat.

Lucchesi says, "Sorry."

The man says, "It's time to sit, folks. Or don't you have manners?"

They sit.

The man says, "What type of food do you have in there? I hope it's American."

Lucchesi says, "Three peanut butter and jelly. Two baloney and three roast beef."

The man says, "Cat got your tongue? Can't say the word sandwich?"

Silence.

The man says, "They call me the Warning Signal, ever since I was knee high to a grass hopper. Let me take a look in there, if you don't mind. Do you mind?"

Lucchesi hands him the backpack.

"What is this, pray tell?"

He holds up a small jar of artichoke hearts.

Ruth says, "Artichoke hearts."

"And this? Is this at all necessary among civilized folks?"

Ruth says, "Sun-dried tomatoes packed in olive oil."

"Never heard of it, but my dog here will eat anything. On occasion, I've seen Dukie eat actual human pussy. Didn't you, you old son of a gun? I don't myself, but then who ever said I was perfect? Only in the eyes of the Lord."

He laughs.

He says, "I notice you're finding it a wee bit difficult to initiate conversation. Can't say I blame you. Let's have some normal talk. What do you do for a living, bub?"

"Used to be a writer. But I'm finished—I'm a has-been."

"That is very sad. And you, dear?"

"I used to be a photographer."

"Two has-beens, huh? Is she your best girl?"

"We're married."

"I said, Is she your best girl?"

"Yes."

"That's the important thing, you know. She should be your best girl until death do ye part. Let me tell you I don't get much pussy. I don't get much ass. A writer, huh? What kind of writer?"

"A novelist."

"Hot dog! You're going to make a comeback, good buddy. Entertain me."

"My novels are not especially strong on plot, but I'll—"

"Don't think I didn't see that awful thing you're plotting to use on me in the bottom of your backpack, fella."

"It's normal for a hiker to have one. I'm not a violent person."

"He talks to me about violence. My oh my. Now sit exactly like me. Good. You too lady. Okay, don't. See if I care. If I was you I'd change out my clothes right quick before I caught the death of a cold. You two birds look like wet rats."

Ruth says, "We don't have a change of clothes."

"Makes no difference to me, hon, unless you have one of those fallen butts. That I don't want to see, if you have one. Do you have one? Don't answer. That's okay. Do you know who I am?"

Lucchesi says, "I'm afraid that we haven't properly introduced ourselves. I'm Thomas Lucchesi."

"I'm Ruth Cohen."

"As I believe I stated quite clearly a moment ago, I am the Warning Signal. I am the Omen. You two birds suffer from Alzheimer's?"

Lucchesi says, "What is it that you wish to warn us of?"

The man says, "Is it proper manners to end a sentence with a preposition? Miss Guckemas taught me it wasn't. Are you saying different? Are you contradicting Miss Guckemas?"

He laughs.

Ruth pulls off her sweater.

"I've come to warn you about nothing in particular."

Ruth says, "Everything in general?"

"Good buddy, your best girl is a real wise guy."

Ruth undoes the buttons on her shirt.

"It's a fact—I've come to warn you about everything in general. Because you two believe that you—button up that shirt lady."

Ruth does not comply.

"You two believe that you can walk with impunity down a no name stream. How the hell did you get that way? I take it back. You two don't believe, because people like you have no feeling for the sacred. People of your ilk just make assumptions. Left and right. But I ask you, Did the martyrs of the early Church make assumptions, or did they believe?"

Ruth takes off her shirt.

"Have the common decency now to give me those three peanut butter and jelly sandwiches. Lady, don't make me mad. Who the hell asked you to butt in here? You've got a lot of nerve. Dukie here wants the roast beef, don't you old fella? Old fart eats me out of house and home. In my opinion, you're not martyr material, not just yet, but go ahead and prove me wrong, see if I care. Put that shirt back on, lady."

Ruth does not comply.

"I said, Put it back on."

"I will not."

"What did you say?"

"No."

"What?"

"Are you deaf, Mister? Are you a deaf old man?"

A terrible silence.

Ruth says, "Now listen to me, because I'm going to tell you a story about everything in general. Is your hearing aid in working order? I have a story in me and I'm going to pour it hot down your throat. Shall I take my bra off, dumbo?"

"I am not such an old man, lady."

"From my mouth into you."

"Is your best girl making me some kind of filthy proposal?"

"Yes, I am."

"Has she any idea what this thing in my lap can do to a woman's pussy? Lady, I am not a dumbo. You'd best be nice."

"Which thing in your lap? One is for killing, the other for fucking. You can't fuck me with your hearing aid, Mister. Or with anything else."

The man stands. The dog stands and growls.

He says, "You think I'm too old for you?"

"No. It's the hearing aid."

The man says, "You'll see. You two have something coming to you, because I am only the Warning Signal. You just wait and see."

Ruth says, "Leave."

"May I at least have those three peanut butter and jelly sandwiches?"

"You may not."

"You're mean, lady."

The man and his dog disappear.

✺

In the Jeep, in a downpour—visibility approaching zero and nothing said between them yet, when a white-tailed buck with a majestic rack dashes across the highway and Ruth brakes and swerves and manages somehow to keep the vehicle on the road.

"Christ," she says, "out of nowhere."

She feels her shirt for the cigarettes she gave up years ago. He looks at her—a kid at last meeting his sports idol. He turns on the radio, loud. She turns it off. He reaches into the backseat and pulls two sandwiches from his backpack. He offers her one.

She says, "Are you kidding?"

He says, "Me neither."

A long pause. He offers her a protein bar—she refuses. Once more, he says, "Me neither." He feels his shirt for the cigarettes he gave up years ago.

He says, "Ruth Cohen saves us again."

"Again? He was a wimp."

"Which you couldn't have known until he crumbled. I was sure you would get us killed."

"You first. Then me—raped and murdered while lying in your blood."

"So you provoke him? Where's the logic?"

"If the provocation causes him to kill us, he's going to kill us anyway. If it doesn't, we're free. So where was the risk?"

"At least you get the satisfaction of going out on the attack?"

"I wasn't about to twist slowly in the wind."

"He wasn't the only wimp. I felt like a spectator at a staged hallucination. Ruth, what a man you are!"

They laugh.

"Did I fail you, Ruth?"

"You did the smart thing. What I did was stupid."

"What you did was courageous."

"I just wanted to hurt him before he hurt us."

"I don't buy it—you're trying to bolster my foundering manhood. You had a strategy. You sensed a vulnerability in the balls. He never had a chance. The Warning Signal. The Omen. It's obvious, isn't it?"

"What?"

"We must not go to Baghdad, saith The Prophet."

"I'm exhausted."

"What are we going to do about Lois Gint's offers? Seriously. We should have a thorough talk."

"After we get home. After we shower and change off—"

"I'll watch you take your bra off."

"After lunch. Then we can have that talk."

"Very nice. What was the story you were going to tell him? The story of everything in general. Tremendous."

"Later."

"Very nice. Yes. I never learned the technique. My shortcoming, one of several, as a novelist."

"What technique?"

"Teasing out suspense."

"I can't tell you how tired I suddenly feel."

"The way you handled the Jeep just now! The way you handled that man!"

"I'm worn out, I'm really worn out."

"I feel a soreness in my legs, as if we'd hiked four miles straight up."

He strokes her hair and says, "I'm a lucky man."

They don't shower. They don't change clothes. They don't eat lunch. They sleep for three hours.

"You had no story in hand?"

"No."

"You were going to make it up on the spot—while this lunatic had his finger on the trigger?"

"As I went along, I'd try to make it up—I would maybe discover my story as I went along. Or maybe not."

"Sounds like the way I write. Out of what, though? You must have had some idea to begin with—some germ of plot."

"The subject was to be the Grenville Sea."

"Never heard of it."

"It no longer exists."

"Where was it when it existed?"

"Here. Covering the northeastern section of what we call North America. Where we were sitting with that man."

"Is that how you start a story about everything in general?"

"I was trying to scare him when I said everything in general. How do you tell a story about everything in general?"

"You say it no longer exists—maybe that's how."

"I don't know—I never had to tell a story."

"Make believe that I'm the man. Try it out on me."

"I'm no storyteller."

He pulls from under the bed the always-loaded shotgun. He instructs her, gruffly, to sit on the floor. She complies. He sits opposite her, weapon across his lap. She reaches over to check the safety latch. It's on. He switches it off and says, "We need to recreate the original crisis circumstance of the narrative. Your life is at stake."

He places his finger lightly on the trigger.

She says, "Good. Keep it there."

He says, "Lady, now see here now. Seas are called the Irish, the Black, the Adriatic, the China, the Dead. They are not called the Grenville. Don't make it up, if you know what's good for you."

She undoes the top button on her shirt.

She says, "When geologists talk about the ancient history of the earth, billions of years before the disease of man, they play Adam and Eve. They become the original namers of original things. They decided to call it the Grenville Sea because they were Canadians who discovered pieces of the ancient corpse in their backyard, in a township in Quebec, called Grenville, where they found rock that was originally deposited in the sea as limestone mud. Those Canadians were place proud."

"How clean the earth, lady, before it was besmirched with our names, when it merely was, in the difficulty of what it is to be."

"I like that, Thomas, very much, but it's out of character. The man could never have said it. Nevertheless, my thought exactly. The earth was a no name place. Remember, about a year ago, when we talked about plate tectonics?"

"Yes."

"Remember I told you about a sea that was closed by an approaching continent?"

"How could I forget?"

"That sea was the one those Canadians decided to name the Grenville Sea."

"Take your bra off, lady."

"I get so rapt, Lucky, by the sight of rock, that at times I feel it would be sheerest joy to become rock."

He says, "Why is it, Ruth, that with my finger on the trigger, when I call you lady, the way he did, when I try to imitate his intonation, I feel a stirring in my crotch?"

"Because," she says, "in the final phase, imagination is everything."

She takes off her bra.

The Geology of Love

About a year ago, we were flattened on an August afternoon at Ninth Lake by record levels of heat and humidity. He proposed that we seek relief in the homeopathic method (his actual words). Afterwards, he rolled over and picked up the 983-page tome on my bedside table, *Geology of the Adirondacks*. To that point, he had shown no interest in my new reading. He shook his head and said, I don't know Ruth, I don't know. Then, naked, he stood and walked around to my side of the bed and said, What has this (holding up the book in one hand) to do with this (with the other hand touching himself). This (touching himself) is the thing itself. This (penis still in hand) is love. We laughed. What has this (waving the book) to do with this (waving his penis), or this— and he dives down quickly and brushes his tongue across my vagina, then crawls over me back to his side of the bed, saying as he crawls, There is, there can be, no geology of love.

Generally, I'm not up to the task of riding his metaphors, but this time I was primed. I say, It isn't true, then proceed to give him my short course on plate tectonics—how continents, separated by oceans, like lost lovers longing for one another, seek each other out. A journey of several hundred million years. The ocean between them closes. The ocean crust, the ocean's very floor, rammed persistently from behind, dives deep down beneath the awaiting continent, thanks to the force of the approaching lover, the propelling and propelled continent. He asks, Continents and ocean floors are in constant motion? Yes, I reply, continents and ocean floors are crustal plates, like large patches of scum, afloat on boiling water, and driven by thermal plumes from below. As the ocean crust dives deep and hard beneath, it produces unimaginable heat and pressure. Volcanoes are thrown up, eager to explode their lava all down the flanks of themselves, flooding the basin below.

What about the approaching continent, the aroused lover, he wants to know? Does it ever make actual contact with the awaiting continent, the one that needs to receive? Does it ever, I say. And the moment of continental collision produces orogeny. (Erogeny, he says?) Crust at the continental margins is crushed and deformed, slabs of the plates override each other, and the crushed crust is thrown up high and folded. This is orogeny, a mountain-building event which occurs when continents come together. Mountains higher than the Himalayas, born hard. This moment, Lucky, this event, a mere punctuation mark in geological time—think of these crazy words, *event* and *moment*, how crazy they are inside the idea of geological time. Plates moving at the rate of two millimeters a year. Think of the extended foreplay. Then the long long withdrawal, at two millimeters a year, the continents separating as a new ocean divides them once more. This entire event of passion, from the moment of initial shy contact—two millimeters a year!—to post-coital afterglow is one hundred million years in duration. Ruth, he says, let's practice long long withdrawal!

I tell him that the metaphor of amorous contact expresses only the force of a desire—his, not mine. I was just playing, I say. Because I remain content with the truth of rocks as they are. He flips through the pages of the book, stopping at the picture of a huge boulder, the size of a small building, resting perilously at the edge of a mountaintop. The boulder has a somewhat darkish cast. The bedrock upon which it rests, and the surrounding rock, does not. He says, Oh, I like that, I like it very much. What he likes so very much is the caption that describes and defines the huge boulder as a glacial erratic. It's the phrase, of course, not what the phrase refers to, that he likes.

Our bodies are wet from head to toe. The yellowing pages of the book that he holds are dampened, and scented, by his touch—by the fingers that have been all over me, and in me. He reads: "A rock transported by glacial ice and deposited at some distance, often great distance, from its geological origin, and resting now on bedrock of alien lithology." Lithology? The study and description of rocks? Yes, I reply, but here meaning the physical character of rocks. The glacial erratic doesn't belong. It's home lies several hundred miles to the north. A footnote informs him of what he, my paramour of the *Oxford English Dictionary*, already knows. That erratic is from the Latin meaning to wander, prone to wander. He reads the final words of the caption: "Alternatively: lonely erratic." He grins. He says, "You're my glacial erotic."

I don't remind him that the erratic was carried by the glacier. Passive voice. That it didn't wander ("like a nomad," his idea). That although it sits alone in an alien landscape, it is not lonely. That it doesn't know it's far from home.

My husband only says, Just like us, Ruth, reclusive in the Adirondacks—far from home. Two deviants from the standard—erratic together. Geology, he says, is good.

❀

Ruth says, "I've made up my mind to go to Baghdad and I'd like you to come with me."

She pours two cups of green tea.

He says, "You haven't forgotten the past and you choose to repeat it? I don't drink tea."

He rises and goes to the cupboard and brings back the box of Animal Crackers. Takes six for himself and pushes the box to her. She pushes it back.

She says, "Drink your tea, Thomas. It prevents cancer of the colon."

He takes a great swallow and says, "You can't afford another Cuba. The ghouls will be waiting for you in Baghdad."

"You're hyperventilating."

He finishes his cup and pours another as he says, "I know why you want to go to Iraq. It's what she said. You'll do it out of love for me, not because you want to take Saddam's picture and not because you can be bought off, though three hundred grand is not peanuts and we need the money for the final phase."

She hasn't touched her tea. He takes her cup and says, "If you're not going to drink this. In a scene of this import, you know, people drink tea as they decide their fate."

"If I'm doing it out of love for you, because I believe in your work, because the commercial shit house of this culture will not give you your due, because this is a chance for your work to receive the recognition it has always deserved—my reason is not honorable? To do it out of love is wrong? How can it possibly be wrong? Better to do it for money rather than love? For fame rather than love? I'm doing it out of love. Yes. So what?"

She takes back her cup of tea and sips. She takes the box of crackers and removes one.

She says, "This one looks like a poisonous snake. It has the triangular head. Do they think kids want to look at this?"

She eats the cracker.

"I can't get the recognition on my own, so I take a ride on my wife's reputation. How am I supposed to live with that?"

"If Pound hadn't pushed Joyce, no one ever hears of Joyce. Pound did it out of love for the work. Just as I do. And out of love for you. Yes. But don't think I can't separate the two. I would love your work even if I didn't love you."

"If you hadn't met me, you would never have read the work. Or even heard of it."

"We know who we are, Thomas. Lois Gint can't get into our heads if we don't let her. How will you live with it? You live with it the way Joyce lived with it when Pound said, Let me help you."

Pause.

"You never saw Kennedy privately?"

"I thought we established that."

"If Saddam or his lunatic sons decide that they like you? Then what? We die in Baghdad, that's what."

"I'm fifty-eight years old, Thomas. You're hyperventilating again. Only you like me, as you so quaintly put it."

"I agree to the Avedon photo?"

"Of course."

"We're actually doing this?"

"There's a FedEx box in Old Forge. I'm going to put two conditions in my response. I'll stipulate that we don't do it unless you have the Knopf contract in hand before we leave. And she must deposit half the money in our account on the day we get on the plane. Confirmation of the deposit to be delivered to us upon our arrival in Amman."

"Do you suppose Jordan calls its national airline Air Jordan?"

❂

On the way to the airport in Syracuse, Lucchesi prevails upon her to stop in Old Forge, so that he can pick up a copy of the latest *Adirondack Weekly*: "Because it'll remind us, when we're far from home, of who we really are, and what we've left behind."

She doesn't respond.

He says, "Dialogue is required."

"Perhaps I don't wish to be reminded."

"What's the name," he asks, "of that funny little man?"

"Which one?"

"Who brought the letters that seal our fate."

"Leon something."

"Leon Szaflarski?"
"That sounds right."
"Listen to this:"

FATAL CRASH IN BOONEVILLE

In a one-car accident yesterday of unknown cause, a man was killed and burned beyond recognition. All personal effects were destroyed in the blaze. State police working out of the Forestport barracks traced the vehicle to a Syracuse rental agency and determined that the driver and sole occupant was a Bronx man, Leon Szaflarski, whose sole surviving relation is a cousin residing in West Orange, New Jersey, which we are informed is in the vicinity of New York City. The cousin stated to the authorities that he hadn't seen the deceased in over 30 years, that he did not know where the deceased worked, who his known associates were, or why he would be traveling in the North Country. According to Captain Natalie Dudek, authorities have no knowledge as to the whereabouts of the deceased prior to the accident. Mr. Szaflarski's painful case, she said, is closed.

After a long pause, Ruth says, "You were right."

"About what?"

"It reminds me of who I really am, and what I'm leaving behind."

II

Utica, New York

1990-1991

She awakens to the sadness that exceeds the old familial causes—the sadness that exceeds its new, its most confusing cause, the exorcist who would cast her sadness out, who looms above her on the second floor of a narrow, ill-insulated two-family house, where only the soft-footed and the whisperers can keep their secrets, here in the heart of Utica's crumbling Italian-American fortress. Ruth Cohen at dawn struggles with the intrusion of sudden intimacy and tenderness, with the man of changes, this exorcist who himself requires exorcism—who had described himself on the day of their first meeting as a "former Italian-American," returned in "the shame of irremediable failure" to his birth place.

Thrice in the dead of night he had tromped the floor of the fragile old house, the floor over her bedroom, like a furious Rumpelstiltskin, thrice failing to wake her, who slept, as always, the sleep of the long defeated, deep and uninterruptible. He, Lucchesi—the intimate intruder—wishes to make her happy. She wants only to live. To live, she tells him, would likely suffice.

"Marry me and have my baby"—the semi-comic refrain of the last month. He's known her for two. He at fifty-nine, she at forty-six—neither thinking frequently enough that they are characters in a comedy. He who says, *Femmina misteriosa*, let me in. You're going to abandon me. She who says, Make love to me instead of this conversation. Now. Who says, Where am I, really? What is the point? Who says, Make love to me, quick. Who says, I'm tired. Who says, No. Who says nothing.

Ruth Cohen has awakened once again to the sadness that exceeds all causes, and to a sound—surprisingly light, almost musical—of descending footfalls. At the bathroom sink she douses her face with cold water. Does not look in the mirror because she has never been interested in her looks.

A tap at the door.

❈

After the espresso, the biscotti, and the loving nonsense—after he says, "You are my sun before sunrise" and she tries, but fails, to beam, and cannot speak, they exit 1311 Mary Street and hit the streets of east Utica to begin the morning rite. He calls it a hike, she says stroll. Outdoors, she feels free.

"Thomas," she says, "you've never been camping and the only time you've seen rural America is from 30,000 feet over the planet. A hike is rough terrain, steep grades, a pleasurable pee in the woods and the levitating fatigue that plucks your mind out. This is not a hike. This is a lover's stroll, where the small danger is when we look lovingly into one another's eyes we step in dog poop, and the fatal danger is excess mental energy. To think about ourselves. To give ourselves pain. Because on a stroll your mind is never plucked out."

"Only the unexamined life is worth living?"

"Only the lived life is worth living."

"We're deep this morning. And unusually loquacious."

She's not smiling.

He says, "Actually, we're hiking the rough terrain of my imagination. We're hiking the vanishing Italian-American frontier. If things go well, our minds will be plucked out. Where is your camera to shoot what isn't here? I'm going to bring back the dead, Ruth, with Utica stories. Give them the lived life they missed the first time through."

"Ghouls," she says.

"Photos by Cohen, text by Lucchesi. Your long anticipated second book appears at last in collaboration with the long-anticipated lover. The obscure writer carried at last into the light by the reluctant and once famous photographer. Anticipation is good. Anticipation produces heat in all the right places. How's your right place?"

She manages a little beam and says, "It's true about the heat, but I never knew there could be a man like you, so I couldn't possibly anticipate you."

"A man like me? With whom am I compared? I'd prefer that you compare me to a summer's day."

She wonders if he's serious. He looks a little wounded.

Apropos of nothing but the *non sequitur* of his anxiety, he says, "We should be sleeping in the same bed. It's not right. The loneliness I go through. The insomnia in the dark. You sleep like a stone, Ruth."

She slips her hand under his shirt.

She says, "Eventually you'll see. It's a good thing to have separate quarters. Think of it as preparation for what lies ahead. This is what love is for. The final separate quarters."

"You believe we crossed paths in order to die well?"

"Yes."

"Not to live well?"

"If we die well, maybe we've lived well."

"Is that what you think love is for? To make us ready to die unafraid? Who could possibly believe that?"

"Unafraid is your word."

He says, "We won't talk about our personal demons. Who needs grievous self-reflection? I take your point."

"I'm safe this morning?"

"You're safe."

"And tomorrow?"

"You believe in ghosts," he says, "I only imagine them."

"I believe in ghosts. Ghouls."

"Who would have thought it? A strawberry blond Jewess, involved with a neighborhood boy, at 1311 Mary Street. Did you say ghouls? Ghouls or ghosts? They're not the same."

She says, "Wait."

They halt.

She says, "It's an incantation, isn't it? 1311 Mary Street. How many times have I heard it in the last two months? You say it and something I don't and maybe can't see springs to life. Your face lights up."

"It's my pin number at the bank. The security code for my credit card."

"Your security code."

"Who am I kidding? I have no talent for bringing back the dead. My Utica stories stink. Who do you flee, Ruth? Who are the ghouls?"

"Your fiction takes my breath away."

"You're kind, Ruth. Now tell me about the ghouls."

"I'm not kind. Not about work."

"You're changing the subject. My fiction is irrelevant. Everyone knows this. You can't tell me there are ghouls in your life and then just drop it."

"I'm brutal about work. You're special. There's another kind of writer in you, but you're afraid of him."

He says, "Let's cross the street. I want to show you something."

She does not move.

She says, "Do you need to change the subject?"

He says, "What about the ghouls?"

"The novelist you flee is a Wallace Stevens of this neighborhood, who *thinks*. Nobody has done it. Not even James Joyce, who knew everything but could not think, or love."

He says, "Wallace Stevens? The insurance man who wrote lyric poems about what? Impossible to say. Let's cross the street."

She does not move.

He says, "I want to tell you a story about a man with a baseball bat. He lived over there. He's dead. Joyce is also dead. Joyce could not think? Are you mad?"

"Joyce's mind was a warehouse. A warehouse is not a mind. You have a mind, Thomas."

She grins. Ruth, ear to ear. He's never seen this before.

"I have a mind and Joyce doesn't. Good. Let's cross now."

She does not move.

"I want to show you something over there. Is he any good? Did he love before death?"

"You know Joyce was awfully good."

"Wallace Stevens. I can't read Wallace Stevens."

"He was terrifically good. Loved his craft. That's what he loved. Loved his craft to death. Then he died. But not before creating mysterious beauty."

"Was Stevens afraid?"

"I don't know. Who knows?"

"Am I dying?"

"Yes," she says, "but not now."

"Cross the street with me and we won't have to have this conversation."

She does not move.

"You love Wallace Stevens?" he says.

"Yes."

"How about me?"

"Are you serious?"

"Yes."

"I love you, Thomas."

"Me or my writing? Be careful how you answer."

She thinks he's funny. She's smiling again. He's not smiling.

He says, "Will I be prepared for death if I love you well? I won't be afraid? Is this your promise?"

"Yes."

"Tell me you love me again."

It occurs to her to say that loving me well doesn't entail asking *me* if I love *you*.

"I love you," she says. "I think we'd better cross."

He does not move. He says, "You can't make that promise to me. What if I don't love you well? You can't keep that promise."

She says, "I promise to love you."

"No," he says, "The other promise, that I won't be afraid."

"Tell me now all about the man with the baseball bat."

He moves, his hand slipping down her back.

He says, "You're a mysterious beauty."

❉

They've been strolling on a Sunday morning at 7:00 in mid-July, 1990, a few weeks before Saddam invaded Kuwait. Highest persistent humidity in years, since his father died. No breezes on the twelfth consecutive day of ninety-plus temperatures in a neighborhood without air conditioners. It makes Lucchesi happy to inhale the perfume of garlic going slowly gold in olive oil and the oceans of fragrance already pouring from the sauce pots of the Italian-American kitchens, unto the fourth and fifth generations, pouring forth since day break. As they cross the street, he says, with a touch of awe, "These people are trees. They're here until the end of the world." The two of them hand in hand in Bermuda shorts. Bermuda shorts on Mary Street? And those colorful tops, especially his.

Too colorful, thinks the ancient woman peering through the blinds of her open window. American clowns. They walk two steps, then talk for ten minutes. They're fighting. Why are they hugging and kissing in the middle of the street all of a sudden if they're not fighting? Who the hell is this Joyce Stevens? Is he stepping out on her already? My husband before he died used to say that after we made love he didn't care if he died. I like to imagine them with all their clothes off because it makes me see my husband with all his clothes off, over me and in me. Every morning, talking a mile a minute. You don't talk that much when things are good. That nice looking Jewish girl looks depressed a lot, and that other one, who I remember when he was born, goes up and down like a yo-yo. He was always moody. They're artists. My husband and I almost never went up and down. We weren't artists. He comes back after all these years and for a song he buys the house of his parents from those quiet Bosnians who brought me food every day, for how many weeks I can't remember after I broke my hip and a month later she moves in and they're right away an item. A Jew on Mary Street! Who looks Irish like the Kennedy brothers' sisters. Who shows up here from God knows where. What's so fascinating about Utica that she had to come up here? What's he doing now across the street with his back to me, with his hands down there in front of him where that thing is, where I can't see what he's doing with his hands down there where that thing is. He's looking down there. Baseball bat? Why did she say baseball bat? Is that the modern word for that thing? She's doing something down there with her hand. My Lord her arm is going back and forth back and forth. Should I call 911? They're singing Take Me Out to the Ballgame in broad daylight! They're running. Good. They won't be talking a mile a minute where they're going—their tongues will be otherwise involved. Good. I wish my husband were here to hold my hand when I go, but it's not going to happen.

They played baseball, and a tight game it was, to the very finish, then lounged a long long time on the field of play, thoughtless—they dozed, and when they awoke, plunged—as was their custom—elbow-propped, face to face, nude—they fell into discussion of irremediable grief, the longings never to be requited. They begin with hers for a pure photography, an art of abstraction, and his for a socially thick fiction of formidable political thrust: each desiring the artistic significance achieved by the other. He speaks, as always, with withering scorn of what he has written, and she likewise of *Cuban Stories*. She says that she could not separate the photographs from what surrounded their genesis or reception in the U.S. Or her reception in Cuba and the U.S. by charming frauds of power. He requests particulars, she refuses. Tell me then about the ghouls, fair is fair. She refuses. He believes her to be confused about the meaning of the word. Ghoul. Corpse-chewer. I know what a ghoul is, she says. But you equated them with ghosts, remember? Ghouls are not, he says, like ghosts, the bogeymen of childhood. She says, There are ghosts who are ghouls. They feed on the living. I am not confused. Who are they feeding on, Ruth? No response. You? Yes, she says, and eventually us.

Larry

Until about two months ago, my practice consisted entirely of old Jewish men suffering from exceptionally enlarged prostate glands—old Jews who do not fear death, whose days and nights are governed by the need to pee and the proximity, or terrible distance, of toilets. What they fear are the long lines emanating from the men's room at the theater. Imagine it, twenty-seven geriatrics who require two or three minutes each to achieve painfully unsatisfactory urination, hunched over the pathetic stream, in a men's room of one urinal and one stall during a fifteen minute intermission. Do the math. I routinely suggest a much-performed surgical procedure that would considerably ease the problem and they routinely refuse, because frequency of urination, and little else, grants form and value to their days and nights. They will not permit "a knife to go down there, Larry." I admire it, the commitment to urological disaster. They embrace their big prostates, they embrace the sleep difficulties, the multiplying hernias, the hearing loss, the skin cancers, the fibrillations, the late onset diabetes—the list does not end—the fallen arches, the acid reflux, the debilitated colons, the rhythmic tootings of a relentless flatulence. They embrace it all.

Be a good boy, Larry, that's the ticket, and forget the afterlife thoughts of those big religions. The One who needs nothing is going to bring us up there just to be nice? Yahweh? Larry, Yahweh is not known for that quality. He does not feel our pain. Be reachable and don't be afraid—because you are not G dash D.

The two exceptions to the old Jew rule are a woman, my sole female patient, and an Italian-American named Thomas Lucchesi, whose disturbing claim is that his blood pressure readings are normal only when I take them. He tells me that his symptoms, whatever they might be, invariably disappear *on the way to see me*. This is a head case of a serious order. I admit it, a very flattering head case, who believes that I am the cure. I am not the cure.

A couple of months ago, I inadvertently played matchmaker at a concert at the College and now they're inseparable. Only yesterday Lucchesi called me at home to request simultaneous full physical examinations, but this I will not do. He said, Why is this a problem? It was the Ciompi String Quartet and I was sitting in the front row directly across from the cellist, not by intention. A man comes over to me full of intensity and asks if he can have my seat because unless he's seated directly across from the cellist he has "difficulty grasping the structure." I have a flash that this man intends to assassinate the cellist mid-solo. The man is Lucchesi. I say no problem and move to the other side of my wife and this puts him, not me any longer, my loss, next to a compelling redhead, who could be my wife's older sister, if she had one. This is a woman you'd like to flirt with, but you won't because she scares you. You don't know why she scares you. It takes Lucchesi about thirty seconds to surmount the aforementioned fear. I admit it, it's me she scares. It's obvious that he would like to grasp her structure. My wife is an Irish Catholic redhead and I assume that she is too. Turns out she's a classic of Jewish history, Ruth Cohen. The head case amuses me—she causes me concern. It's a mistake to think of him as a comic character, but it's a mistake I make, and make again.

For the reception we're jammed into a small room, all the music lovers eager to press the flesh. My wife goes for the refreshments and I find myself crunched into a corner with Lucchesi and Cohen. That's not true—I followed them. I wanted to overhear and my desire was easy to requite. I guess the context when he says The New Modernistic? And she says Yes and he replies Wonderful. The New Modernistic, I'm not making that up, is a very old restaurant on the east side, under previous ownership known as The Modernistic. He's lit up, she looks profoundly pleased in that totally restrained way of hers. This woman is fascinating. The sense I have in her company is of something powerful held back, never to be communicated. There are faces designed by God precisely for that effect because God is kind, when in fact there's nothing special behind the mask, because God is a trickster and the mysterious individuality of human beings is overrated. Movie stars, for example. Actors in general. Teachers, politicians, etc. Writers. Let's be fair: physicians. But Ruth Cohen I don't think is possible to overrate. Limited as my experience of her is, I feel confident that this woman is special. He is too, but he's wide open. His uniqueness and charm lie in his bizarre openness, a recipe for complete disaster in an intimate relationship, I should think. Who can withstand total knowledge of the beloved? Total pain for both parties. We sink in the estimation of the one we want most to be esteemed by. And once that happens.

He notices me. The man is grateful. We exchange introductions and when I say Larry Shapiro both do a double take and she says that my reputation precedes me. He says, Larry Shapiro, the doctor to die for, and we all laugh. She says, Is it true that you don't have room for new patients? I say it's true. My face must have said something else. She's good to look at. She says, You'll take me on then? He says, And me, Doctor Shapiro? I really don't have room. To say yes would be irresponsible. Without hesitation, therefore, I say yes. After, on the way home, Megan says, Gee, Larry, I can't believe you did that. I'm standing there like a goof with two glasses of punch and you can't even introduce me? Don't think I didn't notice you couldn't take your eyes off her. You son of a bitch.

I'm only the side character in their drama, but they'd have me be central. Hard enough to be central in your own family. They think too much of me, especially him. It's not the old Jews, it's those two I take home in my thoughts, to my wife and children. I think too much about her. This is not good. The old Jews say be reachable. Don't be afraid. But I am afraid. Where do you draw the line on reachable?

❀

He says I'll be right back and then rises, not bothering to put on pants or robe—Lucchesi on the half shell, she says, as he leaves the bedroom for his study. Did you think of a revision? she calls out, while we played baseball? As you came? He returns bearing one of the massive volumes of the *Oxford English Dictionary* to find her no longer in bed but at the window, gazing and brooding down over Mary Street, naked. For God's sake, Ruth, he says. She replies, phlegmatic and remote, The light. I'm invisible from the street. He's suddenly aroused. He says, Let's play baseball again in full view. She says, We're hidden behind the glare. No doubleheader. He says, Let's make believe, let's make believe we're in full view. I want to do something in full view. Let's give head doubly. She says, Touch yourself. Do it now. We're in full view. He says, Ruth. She says, Spell it out. I want that you should spell it out what you want to do with your Jewish girlfriend in full view, and let's make believe a teenager is watching from the street. She slides her finger in, smoothly sliding on his semen. Boy or girl, he says? God is in the details. Boy, she says. He says, I want to do what you're doing, let me do that in full view, and let's make believe the boy has been joined by his girlfriend. She says, They both watch us at the window as the light changes, as we do special things for each other, as all of Mary Street sings Take Me Out to the Ballgame. Withdraws her finger. Holds it dripping before him. He says, grinning, Semantics before semen. She touches him, hard in her hand. Volume 6, he says. The "g" words, Ruth. I've just learned something interesting about ghoul. You spoil everything, she says, with your books. The way she says books should scare him. She says, Your semen, and wipes her finger on the book. Take it as my answer, she says, to that word, and all others. She begins to dress. What are you doing? I'm dressing. Why? Because we're through. Through? For the moment. I'm going downstairs. He says, Separate quarters. She says, I'll make you dinner. Let me help, he says. No. I'll call you when it's ready. Let me help. No, she says. No.

❈

Then, over coffee, with desire to ambush her secret, Lucchesi says: "Ghoul: From an Arabic verbal root, meaning to seize. Seize and eat. Come, sit on my lap."

"In the mildest form," she replies, "the ghoul of curiosity—a kind of eating. Curiosity is the cannibalism of mind. I don't want to sit in your lap."

"Nice phrase. I'll use it. The ghoul of curiosity. Ghooooul.

Come, sit on me."

"Mondo Ghoulo."

"To be human," he says, "is to have an appetite for devouring humans. We agree. Writers, for example, are ravenous. Men in love are bottomless pits."

"To be human is also to resist the appetite for it. Or to try to resist the appetite for it. Or to want to make the effort, at least, even as we fail to make the effort."

"Come, sit on my lap."

"I don't want to sit on your lap."

"Refuse to act upon the person of another," he says. "Want as little as possible. Stop the monologues. Then totally fail."

"Angels want only to be near God."

"I think I nurture the appetite. I think I don't want to make the effort to resist."

"I think maybe you do," she says.

"Am I becoming a ghoul? Am I already a ghoul?"

"You're a little curious."

"Won't you sit on my lap?"

"I think that I am very far from God."

The New Modernistic

They made their first appearance here early last summer, glowing like movie stars at the Oscars. Twice a week for dinner at that back corner table, where Joann and I used to have a drink after the crowd left. I fell in love with them—I felt graced by their romance, a little lighter in my mind. Then Saddam has to go into

Kuwait, which I never heard of until he went into it. Now it's just Ruth twice a week and I miss them like I miss Joann and me. Joann went fast. Cancer of the ovaries. I don't know, maybe if I could have given her a baby… I couldn't get up in the morning. I experienced nonstop fatigue. I took breakfast at McDonald's. It must be, what is the word? A harbinger? I figured I had cancer, or depression, or both. Then those two came along Tuesdays and Saturdays and the gloom lifted. It was easier to get out of bed. I flossed. I brought my cologne to the restaurant. Now this television war and I'm worried they might be dead as an item. Now the fatigue again, full time.

She comes in alone, she takes my arm, and I escort her to their special table. I like it that she takes my arm. Hey, we have our fantasies at all ages, no disrespect to Joann. I say, "Always good to see you, Ruth." "Uncle Charlie," she says, "let's cut to the chase. The General is at home directing the war and Tommy is no more." I'm shocked because she never brings up anything in a personal vein. I say, "Generals have to eat, no?" And she says, "The General takes his meals watching TV. He talks frequently and foully to footage of Saddam." I attempt again to inject a little levity. I say, "What does the General do when he has to go peepee?" She says, "When the General has to go peepee he turns up the volume to shattering levels, but in the event of an extended irritating necessity, such as an especially difficult bowel movement, which he complains are more frequent since the war started, or such as eating dinner with me—does he know the difference?—he tapes, because I don't permit the war in my apartment." Have I ever heard her say so many words in a row? It crosses my mind,

Does he tape or turn up the volume when they, you know, or are they slacking off in that department? If Ruth were my girl, by God I wouldn't slack off. I say, "Why doesn't he tape so he can accompany his fair lady to my nice restaurant?" She says, "He's concluded that private time is good. He says he's decided to adopt my philosophy of separate quarters. But before Bush drew a line in the shit he wanted no private time." Another Ruth first: a bad word. I say, "You two watch the war together and his private time is when you come here alone?" She says, "I do not watch the war at any time." I'm scared she's on the verge of exposing more personal material, Ruth Cohen of all people, and I don't want to pursue this inquiry because I have a picture of the lovers which I don't want spoiled with the usual pain in the ass facts of life, which are already seeping in like a dark stain. It's like Joann is dying all over again.

She says, "Have dinner with me, won't you?" "A pleasure," I say, and I wonder how I'm going to put away another one. We both order a spag with big balls, but naturally I don't say it that way in front of her. She says, "Let's drink some wine, Uncle Charlie, let's really drink some wine." I go back into my office and come out with the bottle Joann bought me for our first anniversary. Back in those days a fifty-dollar Chianti. I showed it once to a wine type from the College who comes here all the time. He tells me it's worth five hundred at least. Because what am I saving it for? We were supposed to have it for our fiftieth, but she died just after our thirtieth. Am I cheating? Is it possible to step out on your dead wife? I'm seventy-nine for Christ's sake and I feel like I'm working on an illicit affair. I must be nuts. I say, "Why are you calling me Uncle Charlie all of a sudden? Until tonight it was always Mr. DiStefano." She looks at me with those eyes, I feel paralyzed, and she says, "I don't know why. It felt so natural. Did I offend you Uncle Charlie?" I'm tongue-tied. She is kind. She says, "Would you like to change the subject, is that your desire?" She reaches across the table and touches my hand. She says, "I want to move out, but not necessarily far away. Do you know of anything in the neighborhood that isn't necessarily on the market?" I think I know what she's getting at, and I'm excited. The antipasto arrives, which we never ordered. I say to the waiter, "What is this?" He says, "Compliments of the house." I say, "I am the house, Ronny." He just looks at her and says, "Mr. DiStefano is a shy man." Then he winks. Does he know my fantasy? Does she? She says, "He's a charming man. Now let's do justice to this, Uncle Charlie." Ronny says, "Ah, Uncle Charlie" and leaves. I could kill him. We dig into the salami and peppers. Something that is not on the market is the third floor of my three family house, which I live in alone on the first two floors. Directly across the street from 1311 Mary. Nice location. This is what she has in mind. A soap opera on Mary Street so that the whole neighborhood will know. She's going to put his balls in a vice and I say good for her because if he doesn't appreciate what he has he should suffer. In this conflict I am no question going to side with the neglected lady of our dreams. "He has gone insane," I say, "and you want to move into my house across the street?" She says, "Nice location. Where do you get your roasted peppers?" I say, "You want to live on the floor where Joann and I spent our best years and where I watched her die? Where I go every Sunday morning just to sit there and feel her and me again in the past when we were young and amorous. Because I like the past, I like to feel the sadness of it, I like it better than the present, present company excluded. After I sit there for a long time with my wife in my mind I dust the furniture and wash the kitchen and bathroom floors, regardless no one has lived there for years. I Endust the hardwoods and look at the exact spot on the floor where I made love to her on several occasions because this is what we did on Sunday mornings, we cleaned house and we went wild, when we were young and amorous, and when we were not so young and amorous, and when we were not so amorous in the usual way, when we were old on Sunday mornings, and we just cleaned. Last week I laid out her peignoir set, the one she had on when she died. I laid it out on the bed. Then I laid next to it for a long time." I have never said so many words in a row. When I blurted out those words about myself I didn't know those things about myself. She says, "You take my breath away. My request is inappropriate and cruel. I'm sorry, Uncle Charlie." I say, "I want you to take the apartment. It will be good for all parties, including me and Joann." I'm now way beyond embarrassment, I have nothing to lose anymore and I say, "It crosses my mind, I'm going to be very forward now, that you are in need at this time of an older relative, a shoulder of the male gender, which is why you call me Uncle Charlie." She says, "I wouldn't be surprised." I say, "You want me to talk to the big dope?" She says, "If you were younger, or I were older, we would sweep each other off our respective feet." We giggle out of control for sometime to the point some of the customers are giving us looks. We toast each other. I say, "You know how to make an old bastard feel good." She says, "And vice-versa." I say, "But you are not old. I am old." She says, "Uncle Charlie," she suddenly looks strange, "I'm older than you." I say, "Your Uncle Charlie could tell you everything will turn out good in the end, but I will not tell you that. In the end, things are bad. People are a lot of work, in the beginning, the middle, and the end. I'll tell you what I can tell you. You are the number one girl in the world and at the present time he has a problem. Tell him to go to hell." She says, "I can't." We drink a couple more big glasses. "If I were younger, Ruth," I say, "I would have a crush on you." She says, "And I would be honored. I would be honored even if you had one now, Uncle, though I am otherwise engaged." I say, "If I did have one now you would be honored in spite of the forty year differential?" "I am honored," she says. I say, "No, Ruth. You *would* be honored if I had one, but I don't have a crush at the present time because of the forty years. I'm saying hypothetically, that's all." "If you don't mind," she says, "I nevertheless feel honored at the present time—in the hypothetical sense." "Well," I say, "better not tell *him* because even though he's lost so many of the old wop qualities he's still got the worst one. He's a big jealous wop. You come and live in my house and he will put two and two together. You better be prepared if you come into my house. I am prepared—I own a .357 Magnum." She says, "I've seen a little of that here and there, but I'm not concerned. It's an act. Italian Opera. I admit, an act he likes to get into. I suspect his jealousy causes his faltering passion to heat up, thinking he has competition." "So this is a plan," I say. "You come to my house in order to heat up his faults. Get him away from his new girl, Saddam Hussein." She gives me a look. A small smile. This time I'm not tongue-tied. Two more big glasses. I say, "Okay. I don't mind. In fact, it would be good for all parties. Just do me one favor." She says, "What's that?" Then I shock myself but I doubt I shock her because she has one of those advanced minds. I say, "Feel free, because it will be good for all parties past and present, feel completely free when he comes over to wear Joann's peignoir set." I'm starved; Ronny brings the spag and balls. She says, "He calls this place Checkpoint Charlie."

His romantic feelings must have gotten the upper hand. Because he comes over the night they start the ground assault in Iraq, which you remember the American forces routed them in a hundred hours. They called it off after a hundred hours so that they could call it the Hundred Hours War. He didn't come out of the third floor until the hundred hours were up and he looked like a punch-drunk fighter. The next day I see her with a suit case and I say, "The war is over." She says, "Yes." I say, "So are you going back to 1311?" She says, "Yes." I say, "Congratulations, General Cohen." She doesn't respond. She looks strange. I say, "They didn't get Saddam." She says, "No." "So," I say, "the war isn't really over." When I told her I wasn't referring to Saddam, I was referring to her home front war, she said, "I know what you're referring to. How did you put it, Uncle? People are a lot of grief, especially the ones you care most about." "No," I say, "all I said was people are a lot of work." She says, "I am one of those people too." I say, "The jealousy is not a wop act." She says, "I know." I say, "Do you have all your stuff in that suitcase?" She says, "Yes." I say, "Did you leave the peignoir set on the bed exactly the way you found it?" She says, "Yes." I say, "Good, because now it's my turn."

❉

It was Charley DiStefano who gave her the idea on one of those nights during the Gulf War when she dined without Lucchesi.

"Here," he said, "we feed your belly—there, if you talk to the right man, but only if, they feed your solitude."

He was pointing, forked meatball in hand, to St. Anthony, the flood-lit Catholic church across the street that filled the front windows of the New Modernistic, its massive illuminated cross suddenly oppressing her table.

"The veal scaloppini, with a side of nice sautéed baby broccoli, a specialty of the house. And the crucifixion—specialty of that house. Side by side. That's all I know."

She says, "Uncle, you're talking about the crucifixion to someone named Ruth Cohen. Cohen."

"I know who I'm talking to, do you? I'm talking about the complete meal. I never go on Sundays and I don't keep the Holy Days of Obligation, not even Christmas. I might as well be a Jew. Don't even mention Protestant. Because the crowds nauseate me. I go on Wednesday mornings at 6:30 when there's maybe eight to ten tops and nobody sits near anybody else. Father Michael celebrates in twenty-eight minutes. He does not make eye contact, not even when he gives you the host."

"Is Father Michael the right man?"

"The more people in a church, the worse."

"No God in society?"

"No you or me in society, which is a funny thing to say for a gregarious guy in the restaurant business."

Then he startles her: "I love my solitude, which is why I love to talk to you."

"But a church," she says, "is a place of gathering in His name. How can you ignore the social dimension of the Gospels? Isn't that the meaning of a church? A church is not a hermitage."

"The social? They gather, He goes. Because He is Himself a hermitage. I thought you were a Jew?"

"I'm nothing."

"These Protestants want clubs. But when you go before God you do not go as a club. The best thing in the world is to go into a church when it's deserted. That's when you believe. That's when it doesn't matter if you are a Jew or a lousy Catholic like me, you find your desert, which is your favorite dessert, regardless. You find peace, the meal is complete."

"You're a witty heretic, Uncle."

"Not according to him," and he points to a figure in black emerging from a side door at St. Anthony, "because he's the right man. Don't hesitate. Call him as soon as you can."

"Society is the lie that robs us of ourselves and God? Seek Him in his hermitage?"

"That a girl!"

❉

She imagines Lucchesi telling her that they must live on the northernmost coast of Maine—yes, she says, yes, outside a remote fishing village, where we will pray for constant harsh weather, and their prayers would be answered, because God is good. Stop the writing. Stop the photography. No more television, no newspapers, no radio, no phone. One hundred books allowed. Replenishment of stock not allowed. Mornings kept in perfect silence, afternoons of long arduous hikes, spiced with a little banter, very little, usually about the sleek cormorants flying full tilt a foot over the water, and a few, a very few, well-aimed caresses on the treacherous rocky trail to The Lighthouse and a roaring fireplace in mid-July, where they dine on lobster taken that morning, because the lobster is always taken that morning—brown rice, salad of wild dandelions, beverage of ice water. Shall we have the salmon tonight? For a change? We shall. The irresistible apple pie, baked on the premises that afternoon, will be resisted. Then home, to the cabin with the sagging roof, driven back in the fog by the restaurant owner's son, Derek, an eighteen-year-old who wants to be in love, who drives recklessly because he's infatuated with the redhead in the back seat, because he has seen him, Lucchesi, put his hand under the table, and how she liked it, how she liked it, because he imagines his own hand as he drives, under the table on her thigh, high and inside, he says to himself, high heat inside, as only the star left-handed pitcher on his high school team would have said those words, high and tight inside her panties, who was, in truth, infatuated with the two of them, the ex-writer, the ex-photographer, how Derek loved the sound of ex! He wanted to be like them—weathered, graying, taciturn. Derek wanted to be ex. Then under the afghan, they'll do something under the afghan, or not, probably not, total exhaustion, or shall we a little? Yes, a little. Can I do more? Yes. Do more. More. Overriding their exhaustion, I'm riding you high and inside.

To make love or not to make love, these are their choices on this coast, this hard place with no obstacle between them and the roof-leveling storm bred on the Atlantic, screaming now under the eaves, in her terrible solitude of Thomas. But who is that other beside me if not Thomas, and when no Thomas who then feeds my reverie, who is that other? In the dark, in excited reverie, she imagines the final solitude. Thomas gone. Dead. Who is that beside me then? He who is complete in Himself, but will not let me go. I need to find Him in the waste and agony of stony places, the God of Our Solitude. On a hard coast in Maine, or in the forlorn high desert, one hundred miles west of Taos—surrounded by lightning and thunder, but no rain. Those are her choices.

She wants to believe in God, to be made real by a child's love, or God's, but Ruth and Thomas have, will have, no children. And perhaps not God. Go now and find Him in your despair. (Who speaks to Ruth Cohen in her reverie?) He waits. God the tiger springs in your despair. You He devours. (Who speaks?) She tries to believe.

❉

She could not make the call—DiStefano had to make it for her. On the evening of her interview, Lucchesi put aside the war for his deepest obsession, his ever failing health. When she left, she said, "I'll be at St. Anthony. Talking to a priest." Nothing. No response. He was lost in the report received that day from a gastroenterologist. A report on his colonoscopy, performed at the request of Dr. Larry Shapiro for follow up of colon polyps (benign) seen in

1988. She said, "See you later." After she'd gone, after she'd shut the door with some force, he said, "Ruth, the colonoscopy revealed spasms in the sigmoid colon, multiple large-mouthed diverticula, increased haustrations at the splenic flexure, and two small polyps. Benign. What are haustrations and why are mine on the increase?"

Before him, two pieces of paper, side by side. The cover letter and the formal report. The cover letter stated that the polyps measured five millimeters ("one in the cecum measuring about five mm") and three centimeters ("one in the sigmoid measuring three cm"). Whereas the formal report stated that the polyp found in the cecum "was five mm in size" (not "about five mm") and that the polyp found in the sigmoid colon "was three mm in size" (not "about," not "three cm"). An error in transcription? Or was there, in fact, *a third polyp*, in the three centimeter range? A third *unbiopsied* polyp? Mangled in the polypectomy ("with cold forceps") to the point that a biopsy of it, *the third polyp*, could not be performed? How big, really, was a three centimeter polyp in comparison to one at three millimeters? His understanding of the metric system was shaky. He tended to think in terms of the Richter Scale. An earthquake at 6.6 was what? What did they say on CNN? A hundred? A thousand times more forceful than one at 6.5? Colon polyps grow more slowly, they said, than any other cancer. In the low millimeter range they are almost always benign, they said. A polyp in the low millimeters was growing for maybe two to three years. One in the centimeters was likely a decade old, or more. In the centimeter range, low or not, malignancy, he felt, was certain. And the evidence of malignancy was *botched*. What was his alternative at this point? To request a speculative surgery, at his own expense, so that a part of his colon could be removed? Say a foot to either side of the *totally botched site* of the proliferating malignancy? How many feet of colon would that leave him? And would it matter, how many feet were left, since fatal metastasis would already, long ago, have occurred? The lymph nodes. The liver. The lungs. The heart. Can you get cancer of the heart? Would that be my special destiny? This so-called gastroenterologist is worse than a sex killer. He'd better call Larry. He'll call Larry tonight, at home.

As she approaches the rectory door at 7:30 sharp, she sees a tall, robust man in chinos and brightly flowered short-sleeved shirt standing in the February cold of the true upstate New York. Relaxed. Not a hint of shiver.

She says, "Hello, Father, I'm Ruth Cohen."

He replies, "Michael Collins." Leads her to his study. A crucifix and two chairs. A window open six inches.

He says, "Let's get down to brass tacks."

❋

She returns at 10:45 to find him sitting at his typewriter. Staring at the keyboard. Not typing but miming the act.

She says, "Hey, I'm home."

He says, "Let us assume that one wants to type the word millimeter. How does one type the letter 'm'?"

"See you in the morning."

"Wait. I mean, which hand do you use?"

"Right."

"Yes! Let us assume that one wants to type the word centimeter. How does one type the letter 'c'? Which hand?"

"Left."

"Yes! Unless we assume a two-finger hunt and pecker, which a typist working like a slave at a hospital cannot be. The cover letter was typed by a professional. I have the proof. Look: the typist's initials."

"Can I go to bed now?"

"It wasn't a mistake. Centimeter is not a mistake. Ruth, I think I may be finished."

"Good. See you in the morning."

He rises and embraces her. A deep kiss.

He says, "I lived to know you."

❊

On the day before the commencement of the ground assault, she informs him through the blast of General Powell's press conference that she will be moving out the following morning—into Charley DiStefano's third floor apartment. He looks away from Powell. Makes a visible effort to rise, but does not, or cannot rise.

"Across the street, Thomas, is where I'm going. In other words."

He opens his mouth to speak, but nothing comes out.

She pulls the remote away from him and hits the power button.

"Why," he says? "My God."

"You should know why."

"Why across the street?"

"To give you a hard time in the neighborhood where you were raised. To cause a scene on Mary Street."

"You're declaring war in the open?"

"Did you say war?"

"My God. You're leaving me in the morning."

"On second thought, I'm leaving you as soon as I'm packed."

If he was scared, she thought, he wasn't scared enough, and it occurs to her that his first pained Why? was a response to her killing of the power. My God, I can't watch the footage of the Cruise missile firings.

"Goodbye, Thomas."

He picks up the remote. Like a robot. Hits the power. As she leaves, she hears Colin Powell say, "We will cut the enemy off and kill it."

That night, she dreams of DiStefano's wife and JFK. Joann sits in the kitchen, in her peignoir, saying I don't have any children yet and JFK, standing beside Joann, propped on crutches, says, Miss Cohen, has anyone here seen my son Patrick? Ruth wants to comfort them, but she cannot move or speak.

On the following evening, the ground war fully launched, a knock at her door. In he steps, without a word. Just one step. His suntan faded overnight. Wine-reek.

She says, "There is no television here and no radio. Try not to look crestfallen."

"This is terrible. This is all wrong."

She folds her arms.

"We need to reignite our context," he says.

"Plain English, Thomas. Spit it out."

· 97 ·

"Let's make love. Let's make love now."

"No."

"Our passion is our context."

She says nothing.

He says, "I see."

"You see nothing."

She turns abruptly and goes into the kitchen. He's frozen still in the doorway.

"Would you care for a cup of coffee," she says?

"I care for you."

She says nothing.

He walks into the kitchen, opens the refrigerator, leans in, stares.

"I'm hungry," he says. "This is amazing. There's nothing in here."

"Not to mention milk or sugar. Tomorrow I'm putting in an eight-year supply of groceries. You want a severe cup of coffee?"

Still staring into the empty refrigerator: "I'm not sure yet."

"How about me. Look at me. Are you sure about me?"

He turns, but does not look at her.

"Suddenly I'm living under the Nazi regime of Saddam Hussein? Because I support the President and you don't? Is that it? Suddenly I no longer have the right to my political opinions?"

"I don't object to your politics as such."

He sits. She won't.

He says, "Then what's the problem?"

"You have surrendered to this war like a self-abnegating lover. You're now in a world of shit and I'm not joining you. In a nutshell."

"I see. Ruth is jealous?"

"Ruth is bereft. Your new girlfriend is diseased and don't say 'I see' again or you can go home now."

"This war will soon be over. Like a brief fling."

"And among the mortally diseased will be us."

"Let's put it this way, Ruth. If you don't want to make love, which I refuse to take personally, at least we should have coffee. How about it?"

"I'd like a cup, but I don't want to make it. You make it."

"My thought exactly. I'll make the coffee, then we'll sit here and converse like two people who intend to spend the rest of their lives together."

"I don't want to make love to you. Take it to heart."

"What do you say I go out for pastries?"

"Take it personally."

"Where would you like me to go for pastries?"

"Caruso's."

He's thinking, Carmen Caruso, unlike me, is one of those romantic-looking Italians. Carmen is fond of Ruth. They all are. He's thinking that she's giving him a coded message. He recalls that DiStefano once referred to this apartment as his and Joann's love nest. Lucchesi is putting two and two together. I watch the war and she fools around.

❁

"And then, would you believe it? Carmen refused payment. I find that intriguing, don't you? As I leave, he says, Give my girl a big hug for me."

"Change the subject."

"Iraq. Iraq is my Cuba. This is the subject. A fair-minded person would understand—would be sympathetic. Would want me to have my day as she had her day. I think of it as a day for art. What does this cannoli remind you of? Me or Carmen?"

"Change the subject."

"Basically, one can introduce the tubular cannoli as such, as far as possible, into one's mouth. Or one can insert one's tongue deep into the shell. My art needs a transfusion, Ruth. From history. History is what hurts. You had Cuba. You were there and you found your art. Where was I? In Bloomington, taking a Master's in the history of the English lyric. Becoming an aborted literary critic. No CNN, no live feeds from Havana or the decks of our sexy destroyers in the Florida Straits, as they interdicted and boarded Russian freighters. The Missiles of October, Ruth."

"What do you remember, exactly?"

"JFK's speech. A phrase, really. It thrilled me then and it thrills me now as I remember: 'a full retaliatory response upon the Soviet Union.' To hear our President grimly declare that if a missile were fired from Cuba we would rain down nuclear holocaust upon our enemy. JFK lifted me to another plane. I felt good. But where was I? In a library carrel in Indiana, writing a thesis on Sir Philip Sydney. You were there—I wasn't there."

"You're not in Iraq now, either. You're watching television—you're having fun."

"In Cuba you were seized by the art of political urgency. Ruth, Desert Storm could conceivably transform my cerebral work."

"The other thing that you may do with that cannoli, of course, is shove it up your ass. Are you drunk?"

"Not any more. You haven't touched yours."

"Continue to avoid and you go home now."

Then a long silence. Neither able to look at the other. He takes the cannoli from her plate and raises it as if making a toast. He eats. His strategy of not responding to her anger only enhances her anger. This is a good thing, he thinks. He eats with relish. She needs to get it out of her system. Then we'll get back on track. She'll understand my needs.

Ruth is thinking, He understands nothing. Look at him. How happy eating that cannoli. If we don't reach an accord, we're dead.

He says, "When I think about what I've written, do I see the blood-gouts of historical experience? No. I see the rabbit-like defecations of my incorrigible lyric impulse. On the other hand, when I contemplate your *Cuban Stories* I—"

"Stop this bloated rhetoric! Seized by art in Cuba. A day for art. I am nauseous. The blood-gouts of history. Stop writing—come out of your carrel."

"Have one of these—it'll settle your stomach."

"Go ahead, watch the war and eat cannoli. It's all an intense rush, but tomorrow you'll wake up thirty pounds heavier, you'll look in the mirror and you'll say who am I? Then you'll crash and puke. I did not go to Cuba to experience history. The face that seized me most I never took a picture of. That's the one I remember best. Totally strange: Piercingly familiar: Intimate even. Photography? I don't call it photography. For God's sake, I took a course at Sarah Lawrence."

"You were a natural artist discovering her quintessential *materia poetica*."

"Don't call those people material. A natural artist? Please. I was a college senior without a boyfriend, on a Fall break adventure, just taking a few pictures because I wanted to take the faces home. Flat, plain pictures. Did I know what I was doing? Not really. I did it anyway. Because I couldn't help myself. I've never heard a serious artist, including you, call himself an artist. I stumbled on a barely adequate technique and lucked out and the work turned out pretty clean, because I was too ignorant to muck it up. Some famous fool in New York called it art. I was just taking a few pictures. Eat another one. Go ahead."

"I can't."

"You're right about one thing, though. History is what hurts. Go ahead. Eat the entire dozen tonight and maybe you'll speed the day of your recovery. Or maybe not. Maybe you'll never recover. History stinks, Thomas. It's a playground for monsters."

"Ruth, you were there in the midst of the single most frightening event of the twentieth century and you made *Cuban Stories*. You were there. That is undeniable. Your art made serious contact. I need to tear my work down to the ground. I need contact."

"Put your hands on my breasts."

❉

She won't yield to his desire, or hers—he sleeps on the couch. The next morning he offers to take her to breakfast. She refuses: "If you go out for breakfast, don't bring anything back for me—if you go out for breakfast, don't come back no more, Jack." He believes that the touches of tough humor he's heard over the past twelve hours are a good sign and asks (hoping to add a touch of his own) if she doesn't think that her "conditions of negotiation are possibly draconian." She takes the box of pastries from the refrigerator and places it before him: "Ten more of Carmen's economy-sized cannoli, at six hundred calories per. That should sustain you for two or three more days."

He says, "What about you?"

"I'm fasting."

"Coffee at least?"

"Water—I'm purging, for what I must tell you."

❉

"The face was amorphous—I doubt that I could have picked him out of a police line up, not even a week after our first and only meeting aboard my Air Canada flight from Mexico City to Havana. I was dozing when I felt a hand on my shoulder, a finger brush my neck, and then I heard a voice saying Miss Cohen, Miss Cohen, I am with the Cuban government, I am Luis Sandoval. Please forgive my intrusion. I said, It's okay. He said, We have an accommodation for you in first class. First class for a first class lady. Yes? It is my pleasure. Please. I was delighted to follow him to first class. He said Americans were especially welcome in Cuba at this unhappy moment. That at the highest levels there were serious people eager to extend hospitality to Americans. We would be honored, he said, if you accepted our gift to you. He would assist me through customs and the difficult young men in security in Havana and deliver me into the good hands of Hector Gavilan."

"What did Gavilan look like?"

"Not amorphous. But finally amorphous."

"Sounds ominous."

"When I asked him how he knew my name and when I was traveling, he answered, When you called your travel agent in Bronxville did you not make your ultimate destination known? Do not be decepted by the Republican senators who wish to destroy your young President. I remember decepted. There is a level of sensitive cooperation, he said, between our countries even now. People just like you, who desire accord."

"I found myself suddenly in a secret world and it was exhilarating. The exhilaration of risk, Thomas. Off and on for the previous year I'd thought about applying after graduation to the CIA. This was a sign."

"You saw yourself in an obvious espionage novel."

"In which there is surprising death at the end."

"Titillate me, titillate me mucho."

"Sandoval shook his head and said, You must not be so trusting, Miss Cohen. You would make a very bad intelligence agent. You should have demanded to see this. He then produced an impressive ID, pictures of his wife and children, a picture of himself as a teenager in a baseball uniform, and a Harvard Club of Dallas card. Then he gave me a short, avuncular lecture on the perils of the moment. Especially for young women in a Latin American country. He said that I must be wary of Cuban men. Do not be so angry with me, Miss Cohen, when you return to college and learn that we spoke privately with your roommate. In this moment our countries cannot afford incidents. We needed to check your background. Hector Gavilan, he said, would be a brother to me in Havana."

"And you bought all that? A Cuban agent in Bronxville?"

"I was twenty-one and a half."

"As you said: without a boyfriend."

"He asked me if I liked the New York Yankees. *Los Yanquis*. I said they were my team. He replied that with all due respect to Mickey and Roger, his favorite Yankee was Luis Arroyo, the ace short reliever who was called Señor Stopper, the master of the screwball."

"Arroyo was cunning."

"Sandoval's colleagues knew of his admiration for Señor Stopper and nicknamed *him* Señor Stopper, and when he informed them of his assignment, they asked him if he was going to stop her. He told them he would facilitate me."

"He referred to you as an assignment? He said facilitate?"

"He said, I am an agent in Cuban intelligence. This I do not wish to hide from you, Miss Cohen. It is in our interest to protect you. And keep tabs on me, I said? Yes, of course, that too. I do not hide this from you. Why should you be denied such information? You are innocent, but my superiors are paranoid at this time. And who can blame them? There have been plots to assassinate Fidel. Plots, I am sad to say, originating from your CIA."

"The old honesty ploy. Devious bastard. And you bought it."

"A martini on an empty stomach. The romance of first class. In those days, you could smoke. But not cigars or pipes. What did I know? I lit up my favorite cigar. The stewardess objected. Sandoval whispered something in her ear and she said, It's okay, Miss. I was high and happy and inexperienced. My life at college was so uneventful."

"And a serious male was finally paying attention. This was the romance. I've never flown first class. Tell me, Ruth, are the seats so wide that his leg didn't press against yours? Did you pull your leg away, or did you sit back and enjoy it?"

"Patience, Thomas. I will tell all."

"These are the ghouls, then? Sandoval and Gavilan? Cigars, for God's sake! When did you stop smoking?"

"After Cuba. Then a second martini and I slept the rest of the way. When we arrived I was still quite drunk and a little sick and didn't really register the transfer."

"Of you, from Sandoval to Gavilan."

"Of a small package. A box in plain brown wrapping. From Sandoval to Gavilan. Cigars. I put it all together much later. White Owls. My brand. It was to be a gift from me to Cuba's greatest Yankee fan: Fidel Castro."

"White Owls used to be a co-sponsor of the radio broadcasts of the Yankees, along with Ballantine Beer. A home run was a Ballantine Blast. You met Castro?!"

"A homer was also a White Owl Wallop. The idea was to give Fidel a White Owl Wallop."

"Why would he smoke a cheap American cigar when he had those Havanas? The world's greatest cigar. Not credible."

"A gift from a wide-eyed American girl, corny as Kansas in August. A Yankee fan, like him. The idea was that he'd be taken by the sentiment of the gesture."

"Did Sandoval flinch when you lit the cigar? Was he startled?"

"No."

"A woman lights a cigar and he takes it in stride in the pre-feminist year of 1962?"

"Yes."

"Do you know what that means?"

"They questioned my roommate about my habits. They knew my brand. Now tell me what's going through your mind, Thomas. Be completely honest."

"I don't know. I'm in left field."

"You'd rather not say?"

"I'd rather not say."

"You're possibly thinking who is this woman?"

"Those actual words are not in my mind."

"They put me up in a splendid suite at Havana's finest. Sandoval disappeared and Gavilan escorted me through all the neighborhoods for five days. For five days I took pictures. There were terrific lunches at Cafés in the poor sections and fabulous dinners at the four star restaurant at my hotel."

"With Gavilan."

"Yes. All of it, the room, the meals, on the Cuban government, he said. I saw Sandoval at the end, under a tree."

"What did Gavilan look like?"

"A pretty boy with a strut. He had a way of tilting his pelvis when he walked."

"You noticed."

"Whenever we crossed streets, or moved through crowds, he'd place his hand on the small of my back. He opened doors for me. He pulled out my chair at restaurants. He walked on the street side, invariably. He waited for me to begin eating."

"You noticed and you remember thirty years later."

"He looked at me across the table in a certain way. It was—it was a shy intensity. His hand began to linger on the small of my back. When he said goodnight, he was embarrassed—in a certain way, you know? His face flushed. I began to have thoughts."

"Where was he staying?"

"In an adjacent room."

"With a connecting door."

"No."

"For the Sarah Lawrence senior without a boyfriend, it was true love."

"He was a brilliant actor. All the moves were totally crafted."

"You say now. But then?"

"I was having feelings."

"Then what?"

"On the fifth night he told me we could meet Castro the next day if I wanted. I'd assumed that he was secluded in some fortified bunker hundreds of feet beneath central Havana. But Hector told me—"

"Hector—"

"—that Castro loved the streets, loved to press the flesh, and especially in this crisis wanted to soothe his people with his presence, and every Thursday he played softball at the same field with his huge security detail and the kids of the area. As a member of Cuban intelligence he, Hector Gavilan, of course knew the location. We could show up. We could even play. Castro was a fanatic player. Then without missing a beat he said that his superior officer had an extraordinary weekend home on the ocean, which he wasn't using these days. On a secluded beach. Is it possible that after we met Castro I'd like to accompany him there? Swimming. Barbeque. Mango milkshakes. Is it possible that I would honor him with my company? He said honor. I said I would. I said, But if I'm to meet Castro I must bring a gift. I want him to know that many of us in America mean no harm to Cuba. He said, I have an idea. Those cigars you smoke. He would love a box of those White Owls to remind him of *los Yanquis*. He loves Mickey Mantle. I said, I only brought a few with me. He said, No problem, Ruth. It was the first time he hadn't called me Miss Cohen. No problem, I have a contraband source. I will acquire a whole box of White Owls for you to present to Fidel. He would not ordinarily smoke such things, but from you he will be moved. Especially when you smile it is like sunshine itself. You two can light up together. Good idea? Yes? I said, I can't believe this. He said, I will take your picture with Fidel smoking. Then I remembered that I'd run out of film. He said, No problem. I have a camera. A picture of you and Fidel enjoying your White Owl Wallops. The international press will go crazy. You will become very famous, my dear Ruth. Then I shall cook very special for you at the ocean."

"Give me the scene at the ball field, my dear Ruth."

"Behind the backstop they were barbequing an entire pig since the night before. The aroma was wonderful. It was the custom on these Thursday afternoons when Castro played a seven-inning game to feast on pig and papaya between innings. We got out of the car and approached. Hector was carrying the White Owls gift-wrapped in the national colors. People waved—Hector was known.

There were wolf whistles. Hector said I was truly irresistible. He touched my face. Then he said, *Dios*! I forgot my camera in the car. And I must load it too. He summoned a spectator, a young girl, terribly beautiful, no more than twelve. Spoke to her in Spanish and gave her the box. She will bring you to Fidel, he said. She will tell him what is in the package and who you are. By then I shall be back just in time to take your picture with Fidel as you two light up and inhale with pleasure. Fidel was batting—wearing striped shorts and a tank top. He was happy. When he saw us, he held up his hand to stop the action. He waved us to come close. The girl spoke to him in Spanish. Fidel smiled at me and held out his arms in an attitude of embrace. I hugged him and he kissed me on both cheeks. Then he tore off the wrapper and roared with approval. One of Fidel's men approached, took him aside and spoke with enormous animation. When they turned back to us, Fidel was suddenly shielded by several men with drawn revolvers. I turned to call to Hector, but the car was gone. The man who had taken Fidel aside spoke to me in English. He said, We would like you to have the honor of smoking first. I said, Okay and took the cigar he handed me. I put it in my mouth as he flicked his lighter. Then he said, No. She will be first. Yes, señorita? He was pointing to the little girl. He had a puzzling malicious grin. I said, She's too young, don't you think? To honor Fidel, he said, she will do it. He said something to the girl and she smiled and jumped up and down. He placed the cigar in the girl's mouth, then took one of his own from his shirt, lit up, inhaled deeply and blew out with great pleasure. He said, *Si*? She said, *Si*! *Si*! He lit the girl's cigar. She inhaled and died in foaming convulsions before my eyes. Late that night, my interrogator said, You are an American fool. You know nothing. Now follow me. I am going to give you a Cuban memory. He led me into a small harshly lit courtyard where Sandoval and Gavilan were tied to trees. We were within fifteen feet of them. Maybe less. They showed me no recognition. I remember the walls. Pock-marked. Pink and yellow. Two men wearing hoods appeared with baseball bats and proceeded to smash their faces beyond recognition. Chunks of brain flew. I felt drops of rain on my face, but it wasn't raining. On my lips. My interrogator turned to me and said, How do you like your White Owl Wallops now, Señorita Cohen?"

It is difficult to determine which of the two is the more horror-struck. He who hears it for the first time, or she who tells it for the first time. He speaks without emotion.

"I'm sorry."

"I know you are."

"My ideas are stupid."

No response.

"Your art died in Cuba."

No response.

"But you didn't."

No response. She can't look at him.

"Now you desire an art of abstraction, free of the human face."

No response.

"We're here. Ruth, we're here."

She turns to him. She says, "I'm not here."

❈

Larry

They were to receive honorary degrees for their contributions to the arts. Lucchesi had come back to Utica a month before the ceremonies to take notes for a novel about his hometown and decided to stay. He said a male novelist is driven by nostalgia to return in his imagination to the place of his childhood. Nostalgia motivates the work. When I suggested that his nostalgia would be drained off now that he'd actually returned (I offered the analogy of the inserted catheter) he replied that a novelist is the kind of person who longs for his home even when he's there.

She also had come a month before the ceremonies, in order to supervise an exhibition at the Art Institute of the photos that had made her reputation long ago. She too decided to stay—to disappear, as she put it, "somewhere in the vagueness of upstate New York, like the screwed up psychiatrist of Fitzgerald's worst novel." Americans tend to believe, she said, that upstate New York is a reference to the north Bronx. (The melancholy lady has a nice sense of humor.) When I asked which Fitzgerald novel she was referring to, she replied that artistic failures ought never to be mentioned by name, that we dishonor dead writers by reprinting their failures, as we have for so long dishonored Fitzgerald.

I asked her to sign a copy of the seventh reprinting of *Cuban Stories*. She wrote, "To Larry, This lie." I asked him to sign a copy of his first novel, *The Prostate Dialogues*—in the pages of which I found no mention of the vile gland. Beneath his signature he inscribed a snatch of dialogue—from a Poe story, he told me:

"As for Luchesi—"

"He is an ignoramus..."

I said, Astonishing that you of all people should leave out a "c." He said, Poe wrote it that way. What did Poe know about Italians, Larry? He added, I'm abandoning my Utica novel because I've discovered that I also know nothing about Italians. During their year and a half in Utica, on several occasions I caught glimpses of them in the throes of cold-blooded self-loathing for what they had made, at such dear cost, and I thought, A good thing they have each other. A very good thing. What will either have when the other passes?

In a week, they're going off to the North Country, the ultimate vagueness of New York State. Not for a mountain vacation during the leaf change, but permanently. I thought all summer about throwing a farewell party, but now it's impossible. Six weeks ago, Charley DiStefano suffered a major stroke. He's confined to a chair and can no longer speak. He won't recover. Then there was that spectacular old lady, Rose Mattia. I would have invited her, what a wild card she would have made! She lived a few houses away from them on Mary Street. They told me that they knew she watched them on their morning walks. Lucchesi told me that they once mimed a masturbatory act for her in such a way that she must have thought they were really going at it. The old lady gave them a sense of being in theater. They were her theater, and they enjoyed performing for her. Two weeks ago, Rose was killed crossing Bleecker Street. Ruth mentioned Father Michael once in glowing terms, and Charley always talked about him, but he accepts no invitations. That leaves Megan and me. In other words, that leaves me. Megan seems to have come to her senses. On the other hand, the reservoir of jealous rage is always bottomless. Rare in a female, of course, but when it occurs, worse. I wouldn't have wanted to put her to the test.

I like to imagine the seven of us—Rose, Charley, Father Michael, Lucchesi, Ruth, Megan, and me—sitting around our big round dining room table, with the gleaming glass top. How happy we are to be in one another's company. We find each other's face in the glass, but never our own. Father Michael says, "It's pleasant to be in company, what a shock!" We find each other very humorous. We're happy even as unhappiness begins to seep in—as we're shadowed by the sense of an ending, as the evening draws to a close.

Instead of a party, I offered them physicals free of charge—I did not mention this to Megan. They had back-to-back appointments, starting with him. That was in July of '91. The first thing he said was, Larry, do you have any patients who drive in from the Old Forge area? I said, No and he said, You do now. In September we're moving to Ninth Lake. I said, Never heard of it. He said, It's there. Now look at this. He hands me an obit from the *Times*. John D. Rockefeller VII, of natural causes, in Clearwater, Florida. He said, Skip to the last paragraph. Secluded summer property in the Adirondacks left to Ruth Cohen, famed artistic photographer of the early 1960s... He told me that they'd contacted people in Old Forge who specialize in building log cabins with all the conveniences. They'd be ready after Labor Day. Then he says, like a kid, Guess what, Larry? Yesterday we were married by a magistrate at the city jail. Two guards for witnesses. I congratulated him, told him I was happy for them both, and I was, but I was also discomforted by the news, even pained a little—feelings that I managed, of course, to hide. I wasn't in love with her, not really, but for some reason I wanted her to be in love with me.

He said, At one time she knew men in high places. I wouldn't bite. He said, That's what I have to live with. I don't bite. He says, Why else would he leave her the property? Because he loved her art, I say. Those Rockefellers have always supported modern artists. Nice thought, he says, but don't try to console me. At the end of the physical, he says, Do you think I'm losing my hair? I say, You still have a good head of hair, Thomas. He says, Why did you say still? I wouldn't want to lose it, Larry, because writers tend to have nice hair. I tried to think of a major writer who didn't. I say, There's that picture we all know of Shakespeare. He didn't have much and what was there looks awfully lank to me. Then I say, Think of Jackson Pollock. Okay, okay, he wasn't a writer. But we all know how terrific he looked with nothing at all up there. Think of Pollock. Think of Yul Brynner. He says, If I have such a good head of hair, Larry, why are you trying to console me with these examples? He says, She's having some trouble with her heart. I'm scared, he says. It's unlikely she'll mention it, but I depend on you to take care of my wife. When he said "my wife," I felt another pang.

She sits down and I say, I'm happy to hear that you and Thomas were married. Can't say I'm surprised. I'm happy for you, Ruth. Hey, I was the matchmaker! She smiles like I've never seen her smile—the sun has finally broken through. Then I say, Thomas tells me that you've had a cardiac issue lately. She says, It's nothing. He exaggerates all health issues. She tells me that on occasion she experiences rapid heartbeat. For how long? A few seconds. Sometimes a couple of minutes. A week ago, about an hour. I tell her that a few minutes is not nothing. That an hour is serious. I schedule her for the standard tests, all of which tell the same story: no problem detected. So I have her hooked up to the Holt monitor, which is a portable electrocardiogram machine, for a forty-eight-hour period. I asked her to keep a diary and note any episodes, the time of occurrence, and any symptoms. She returned three days later with a blank diary. The Holt monitor showed three disturbances: one for thirty-two seconds, one for four seconds, and one for forty-seven minutes. When I brought this evidence to her attention, she said, Really? I felt nothing. I said, It's true that we all occasionally have speed ups of a very short duration and don't even know it. That would explain the four-second episode. Thirty-two seconds is hard to ignore and a cardiac event of forty-seven minutes impossible. She only says again, I felt nothing. I said, Fine. But you have a problem. There's medication for this sort of thing. It will help. If we have to, there's an excellent device out there called an implantable defibrillator. It works very well. That's our back-up. She replies, I'll think about it. What could I say? A woman only in her late forties, who has just been happily married, should take care of herself? Could I say, Do you realize you are playing with your life? Why would you want to do that? I only said, If I were you I'd avoid extended periods of strenuous exercise. She replied, In the Adirondacks, I'm told, there's great hiking.

Before they left town, I saw them twice for lunch. I saw him at the clinic once for an imaginary illness, a Lucchesi specialty. He said, The dead weep for joy when their books are reprinted—that is my hope for death. Ruth Cohen made no further appointments.

III

Baghdad and Ninth Lake

There he is at last, bemedaled and beribboned in military dress—the grimly confident warrior, Saddam Hussein. There again, earnest and open-faced in traditional head dress and robe of the countryside—Saddam Hussein, peasant-farmer. And over there, in chest-hair baring white sports shirt, white ducks and sunglasses, rakish, deeply tanned at the wheel of his fabulous yacht—the movie star, the secret crush of every Baathist (men and women alike), Saddam of the killer smile.

In this windowless reception hall at Saddam International—where disembarked passengers contemplate their fate at the crisis of passport control—all is awash in dead light, with the exception of the brilliantly illuminated, twenty-by-sixteen foot, four-color posters of the Great Exception Himself, who shall not be underlit. Moving roughly among the passengers, numerous burly-bodied men in black leather jackets—mustachioed in the style of Saddam—talk furtively into their lapels.

A jacket approaches the two bedraggled Americans: "Your passport, *vaya con Dios*." A glance. "I keep passports for control, no problem, just to control you. I am Mahmood al-Sayyid, your facilitator. May Allah spare you, Señor and Señora! How horrible you look!"

Lucchesi says, "Mahmood, I must inform you that we are not fucking Spaniards."

Mahmood replies, "I am laughing, okay? Mahmood is a sense of humor. Laughing is permitted."

He opens his jacket to reveal a snub-nosed revolver holstered to his belt. He says, "I am saying this is not a sense of humor."

Ruth says, "I am laughing, okay? Ruth is a sense of humor."

Lucchesi says, "Be careful."

Mahmood caresses the revolver.

Ruth says, "May I borrow that for a moment?"

"My dear friends, no more shitting, I am saying. The shitting has ended. Are you ready for Customs? Because at Customs, you will be tested. At Customs, they will screw Saddam himself."

Stationed along the walls, their AK-47s held jauntily at the hip, and pointed toward the passengers, teenage soldiers—looking for adventure.

❂

One year later, Ninth Lake.

She's thinking, It would be a nice thing to have, a dog. Could call him Lucky. Or a cat. A cat might be even nicer, who'd jump up on the table and lie here on these photos spread out before me, so much the better to warm them, though she prefers that they remain as they are, like her drafty mountain cabin on this drizzly November night at forty-one degrees, whose stove she refuses to fire up. In panties and bra—cold, wanting to be cold. (Cats are cleaner than dogs.) Photos not of Saddam but of Lucchesi—shot over the years from the platform. Photos of her man of changes, who had no idea she was shooting him. (Cats are aloof.) How hopelessly human these photos are, which is why he would have liked them, as would have the legendary art critic he always sided with when he wanted to tease her—the art critic whose single, pontificating sentence about her "noble reticence" had assured the high place of *Cuban Stories* in the history of American photography.

Storytelling is her grief—exterminate the impulse. Banish the pictorial. Expunge allusion. Suppress the urge to send messages. Annihilate all context. She would look at the world through the eye of her camera and see no worldly significance, no resonance of life. Look at landscapes, and faces, but see only the lurking beauty of the severest geometry, deprived of the consolations of the curvilinear. Beauty fleshless, absolute.

Ruth Cohen believes that she has totally failed, that these photos mock her desire. Because this is what she sees: Lucchesi stories that only she can tell, if only she'd retrieve the context. She's assaulted by memory: Contaminants of the living: Can't have one without the other, Ruth. For example, me. She remembers: Rescue me, *bonita*, from this shit of politics.

They find intense affection painful. When they play, they claw and draw blood, because they can't bear very much attention. Cats. Shedding fur everywhere. She remembers: You'll betray me. After I'm gone, as you did before we met. You'll go to bed with another man. After I'm dead. (These photos, these images of her desire for what is not.) Maybe a dwarf rabbit, because they live in a cage, where their shit is contained. You refuse to give it a name. You pet it, hold it for a while, then put it back in the cage, where it belongs, nameless in its cage, in the spare room. Cats need less affection than dogs. Rabbits less than cats. Rocks need nothing—the rapture of rock. (These photos, this companionable pain.)

She remembers: I'll be back late. Mahmood is taking me to a seedy restaurant on the Tigris. A restaurant with a dirt floor. I'm thinking the experience might jump start my stalled writing. My stalled life. (She hears, in the ear of the mind, my stalled wife.) They club the fish to death with a monkey wrench and grill it before your eyes, guts and all. Or for maximum freshness, they pull it with a long-nosed pliers, live from a tiled tub of water, drive a sharp-pointed skewer down its throat and out its bunghole—then grill it, writhing, before your eyes. Mazgouf. A Baghdad specialty. Come with me, won't you come? She said she wanted to be alone in their vast, traditional Baghdad house. In the silence of the harem.

I asked Mahmood, How do you say, in Arabic, I like to give my wife head? He said, It is not possible, Mr. Lucchesi, to express, or to perform, such a thought in the Arabic frame of reference. Because such an activity defiles God, who abominates the filth of women. If such words are said in Arabic, they signify that someone has chopped your head from your torso and presented it to your wife as a political statement. This is how we give head in Baghdad.

When I return I'll give you head in the harem. We'll defile the culture. Don't go to sleep before we go to bed.

She spends the night in his cabin. In his narrow bed. The next morning, returns to find her cabin ransacked—a window smashed, the mattress upended and exploded and strands of coarse, greasy black hair in the disheveled sheets. Her violent new lover, who unlike Ruth did not sleep well. The table of photos is alone untouched—the photos are arrayed exactly as she had left them. Turds on the floor. Mementos of a needy Adirondack Black bear.

She knows what she lacks and finds it in a second hand furniture store in Old Forge. Cracked wide down the middle—a freestanding full-length mirror.

Ruth Cohen has a plan.

❂

In the room reserved for those who will have direct contact with Saddam, the contents of their two bags are spread meticulously out on a long table, where a uniformed woman in surgical gloves is picking through the various items. She deposits Lucchesi's big-buckled cowboy belt in a metal box. Closes lid, cranks lever. The box hums and vibrates.

She says something. Mahmood translates: "Thank you very much, we have problem. The belt is declared innocent, the camera equipment hanging on the body of Ruth Cohen is also acceptable, but the backpack on your back is causing concern. In this room, we are investigating desire. Have you come to Iraq with a plan, she is saying?"

Ruth places her Leica in its strapped case, the tripod bag, and the large camera bag on the table—Lucchesi does likewise with the backpack.

The woman erupts.

Mahmood says, "She did not ask for Ruth Cohen to do this, because camera things are necessary for Saddam, we know this for three weeks. She is saying if the woman does another irregularity the gentleman who is totally expendable in Iraq must return to where he came from and the lady will stay to consummate friendship with Uday Hussein. You know Uday? She is saying camera things were properly investigated in Amman by Iraqi special agents, we know this, but the backpack formerly on your back must be understood completely. Dangerous people have infiltrated our country from your country, why should you be trusted, she is saying and I am agreeing, my dear friends?"

Lucchesi opens the backpack and reaches in, but she pushes his hand away and pulls out a copy of *The Prostate Dialogues*, inscribed "To Saddam Hussein, Fellow writer, may he be free from the concerns of this novel—struggle against chronic illness is *fatal*." She says, "Permitted" and takes out his toiletry case, unzips it and removes a small baggy of ear swabs, which she promptly deposits in a garbage can ("penetrating devices"), then three vials of medication, a tube of toothpaste, a homeopathic nasal spray decongestant, a jar labeled Tucks, a toothbrush, a second (and larger) baggy containing eighty vitamin tablets of ten different kinds, four large bottles of Advil, a compact labeled Laura Mercier (because "I am a new, gender-flexible male"), an economy-sized tube labeled Personal Lubricant, two large paper clips, and another economy-sized tube, this one labeled Preparation H.

She deposits the toothbrush in the garbage can. Says something to Mahmood and makes a note. He translates: "She is writing to higher authority that you bring no toothbrush to Iraq."

Lucchesi says, "Very nice, bitch."

Ruth says, "Better make her happy, Lucky."

The woman speaks at length, Mahmood responds to her in Arabic. He translates: "Her cousin in Haifa Street sells lovely toothbrushes. Cheap. $12. I tell her you will buy five from her cousin in Haifa Street. That you will give her $60 (no dinars, please) to pass on to her cousin in advance of your visit to her cousin, to save time when you go to Haifa Street. Be happy, we are saving time. Give money to me, I will pass it to her in private. Thank you, Señor. The paper clips are No. She is suspicious of theoretical medications. Unsatisfactory explanation leads to special interrogation in special room with interesting interrogators."

Lucchesi responds, sadly, "This is for blood pressure, this for sleeping, this to help ease the urine."

Mahmood speaks to the woman, the woman replies with poignant eagerness. Mahmood translates: "She desires to know if pills for urination are useful for women because she is having such a problem you would not believe. I cannot survive much longer, she is saying."

"Does she have an enlarged prostate? Mine is the size of a basketball."

"Tell her to see a doctor—she has a bladder infection, the affliction of our gender."

"Under sanctions, only wealthy see doctors."

Ruth takes from her camera bag a vial of medication and says, "What every female traveler must not leave home without, my reserve of sulfa." She presents it to the woman, saying to Mahmood, "Tell her this is for the gender that lacks a prostate." The woman touches the shoulder of Ruth Cohen, the compassionate.

"Tucks. What is Tucks, Señor?"

"For hygiene in sensitive areas."

"Under sanctions, she is saying, her cousin's wife in Haifa Street is in need. Not for herself."

"Give her the jar and tell her not to be profligate at any given sitting."

"And Preparation H? Can this mystery be revealed?"

Lucchesi explains. Mahmood's pocket dictionary does not help. Lucchesi proceeds, as if he'd long prepared the moment, to make a series of sensational gestures.

The woman speaks plaintively.

"She is saying the H problem of her cousin's mother in Haifa Street is completely enormous."

"Tell her when the ointment is used up she should take a very hot bath daily for twenty minutes."

"She is insisting she herself lacks H problem. For her cousin's mother only."

Ruth says, "Dr. Lucchesi will apply it with his highly practiced finger. If she likes, as an alternative, he'll apply it deep with his dick. Tell her to request the alternative."

Mahmood forwards the message *in toto*. The woman blushes and laughs and says something. Mahmood says, "You are both extremely kind, you cause her to forget herself with such nonsense, welcome to Iraq and have a nice stay in Baghdad. We are watching you always. Especially the gentleman, who is totally expendable in Iraq. One more question and you may leave. Who is Laura Mercier?"

"An advanced formula concealer for the acne of my golden years."

"A consequence," Ruth adds, "of an excess of semen, backed up in his system. He can never get enough out, though he tries."

"She is saying that she would like to meet such a man, were he a Muslim, but under sanctions the supply of semen in Baghdad is very low."

Ruth says, "I like this bitch."

"She wishes to communicate that this bitch is a very big sense of humor, just like new American guests and youngest brother, Mahmood. Goodbye, may Allah bless you—and almost all of your countrymen. Mr. Lucchesi's drugs will be mailed to the United States when Mr. Lucchesi leaves Iraq."

Silence—the woman is smiling a fetching smile.

"You cannot confiscate my medications. That is a serious matter. Please."

"She is saying she is in complete agreement. There is time for comedy and time for seriousness. We have reached time of seriousness. So-called medications must be analyzed by Iraqi scientists. The buffoonery of Haifa Street is finished."

"This is outrageous. She cannot take my medications."

"She is saying if she wishes she can take you."

"Give me my medications back, I implore you."

"Mahmood is advising that you have no power."

The woman smiles, she winks.

Ruth says, "Forget it. In a week we'll be home. You can do without for a week. You'll live."

"She is saying you will leave Iraq when Saddam wishes. You will take pictures as Saddam wishes. You will live if Saddam wishes. You have very big toiletry case, congratulations. But in Iraq you are nothing. How do you like your brown-eyed bitch now, Mr. Lucchesi? She is saying."

On the way to the car, Mahmood asks about the camera. So small for such important work. Ruth explains that this Leica is splendid precisely because it's so light, so sleek and unencumbered, so sharp even without a tripod. Such qualities permit total freedom—maximize opportunities for spontaneity. She can move with the unposed subject. There is no moment with her Leica— Germany's smartest weapon of mass destruction, she says—that is disadvantageous for shooting Saddam—rapidly, repeatedly, and at will.

"Yes," Lucchesi says, "the Leica M6 is a thing of beauty, and a joy forever. Quite deadly."

Mahmood does not reply. Instead, he presents each of them with a special gift from Iraqi Airways—a watch displaying the happy face of Iraq's first mouseketeer: Saddam Hussein.

❂

Thanksgiving morning, the gray light of overcast, and she's decided not to wear his watch cap, because neither did he on that hard bright day in January, long ago, when he sat there, huddled into himself, making notes on his long dead, his recessed father. Father of the averted gaze. Lucky sat exactly here.

She's standing bare footed and defiant in the iron cold, looking across the lake at the mountains, which have gone mostly brown, in this light virtually black, and utterly dumb.

Five feet from the water's edge, his metal folding chair (here, he sat, exactly here). Skims of ice, formed and thickened in the shallows, inch imperceptibly toward the deep and Ruth Cohen feels the wind knifing easily through his winter jacket, his heavy cords, his union suit, and she is reassured.

She remembers: Ninth Lake is wrong, Ruth. Solitude and silence are wrong. We were not meant to be monks. This is the message of Baghdad. I've been wrong about everything. This is what I'm learning in Baghdad—that life in a remote natural setting, however beautiful, is desiccation and death.

Come, January, my landscape of ice.

She sits, lost in his clothes—like Macbeth in Duncan's, as jays swoop and scream behind her. It faces the chair on uneven ground. It tilts right, the freestanding full-length mirror.

Come, January, and be my love.

From the manila envelope, the appropriate eight by ten—the one of him shot on that day, sitting here, where she now sits, where he took notes, bringing against the sub-freezing temperature of January a distant happy day in August, at the Black River camp, when he and his father played bocce with Tom Biamonte (then ten years younger than himself at his moment of recollection) while his mother and Rose Biamonte prepared the Sunday meal—was it ravioli? It was, how delicious it was, and a salad of tomatoes and cucumbers fresh from Tom's garden (Tom is dead) and two lemon meringue pies. The beautiful Rose Biamonte is dead. As is his mother. Tom Biamonte—remember, Ruth? The story I never told about the man with the baseball bat. He entertained the kids on Mary Street, even the girls were fascinated by his dead-on imitations of the batting stances of the Yankees of the

1950s. *Who me now? Yogi Bear! That'sa who! Who me now? You no know? Why you no know?*

Studies the photo and glances many times up at her tilted reflection, the off-centered woman in the mirror. She'll start with the feet. Checks the photo, checks the mirror. The feet are easy. Ruth, how tall is Saddam? She's arranging herself, sculpting her posture. The head tilt. Check photo, check mirror. The head is easy, I feel nothing. Does Saddam suffer from middle-aged spread? How many passes has he made? Do you return his smiles? Tell the truth.

From the jacket, a pen and small notebook. She'll put it all together. Pen poised over open notebook, head tilted slightly right, Lucky staring out at the lake and leaning, glazed, elbows tucked in, pigeon-toed, awaiting the seizure of time past, incarnated in a sensuous phrase, words (futilely pursued) that say, Cut me and I bleed time. She leans, she wants to lean in the direction of an elusive image, some flashing thing yet to be disclosed, just as he'd leaned that day in January, pen poised, toward a moment in August on the swift-running Black River, after the meal, when the women washed dishes and old Tom dozed (old Tom!) as he and his father sat close in the sun on a patch of struggling grass, with a transistor radio between them, listening through the static to the fading signal of a ballgame at Yankee Stadium—the feared Tigers of Detroit in town, with The Yankee Killer, Frank Lary, on the mound.

The cracked mirror splits her down the middle—in the outsized clothing her image is amorphous. Only the positions of feet and hands match what she sees in the photo. She feels nothing. I am a heap of borrowed clothes.

Joseph Stalin at any time and Omar Sharif in *Dr. Zhivago*, is what Saddam looks like, she'd responded. And he'd replied, Beauty and the Beast seamlessly blended in a single man—that's the secret of his charismatic power. A rare and irresistible combination. Did you resist? The restaurant is on the broad and muddy Tigris of no refreshing breezes, in the district of neon, and middle-aged strippers, who will say to me, Okay John Wayne want fuckey fuckey or lickey suck? Okay? The room will be full of perfumed and berobed Saudis in checkered headdress, who consult their palm pilots and then make arrangements for lickey suck *only*. And a bevy of slim and sleekly tailored Jordanian homosexuals on a night out at the heterosexual zoo, whose interest in lickey suck must be satisfied elsewhere. Daily I hit the wall of Arabic sound—incomprehensible and therefore consoling. A little like you, Ruth.

Cannot inhabit him. Can't bear this cold much longer, though I want to bear it a long, long time. Like a snowman.

As you work with Saddam, I stroll Baghdad and approach people to ask for directions and they hold up their arms as if to ward off demons and scurry away. Pedestrians and shopkeepers respond to my approaches by stating that their English is not exactly good, my dear man—without a hint of accent. These Iraqis I meet seem to think that a chat with me is the inside track to the electrodes and the dungeon. A woman shielded her baby—from what? My deadly gaze.

(These descriptions you bring me of Baghdadi life sound like writing. I *am* writing. Ruth! I'm writing again!)

She can bear the cold no more and retreats to her cabin, trailed by his account of the climactic moment of that ballgame. Ruth is empty, except for a voice in the head that's saying, The dreaded

Frank Lary had mastered the Yankees once again, allowing one run and two hits. The Tigers have scored three. In the bottom of the ninth, with two outs, Lary falters, or fakes faltering. He was faking. A walk and a hit batsman and now Mickey Mantle is striding to the plate, to do to Lary what he so richly deserves to have done to him, before a crowd of 67,000. The signal is weak, the static dense.

She sees it now at last, as she sculpts his time past out of the haze of that August afternoon. The elusive image: The father saying—what? What should the father say? I'm sick and tired of this Lary. The son saying, Me too but Mickey never hits this guy. Lary is invincible. He's raising our expectations on purpose with the walk and hit batsman, he's toying with us, Daddy, so that he can crush our hearts when he strikes our mighty man out. Lary is cruel.

Young Lucchesi holding the radio up between them, the two heads leaning over the tiny speaker—this is how she wants it—the heads curling toward one another, almost touching, now touching! and the signal strengthening just because the heads touch, that's it, only because they touch the static disappears and Mantle gets a hold of it and drives it far and high into the bleachers. And the Yankees win. And their hearts were made glad. (He thought it was about baseball.) And their hearts were made one.

In her cabin, as she crawls into bed with his clothes still on, pulling up the covers, she saw what he'd never seen. What he'd never see. He who once said, We speak so often of my parents, so rarely of yours. I wonder why. Who are you, Ruth Cohen? Who are you, really?

She's well covered-up.

❂

The sun dies on the Western horizon and darkness gathers fast—like a gloom condensed and motionless, brooding now over the ill-lit towers of the ancient place, the fabled city in the desert. Mahmood swings his government issue, late model Mercedes in the direction of Baghdad.

A big sky, like the sky of the American southwest. Palm trees. Bone-dry air. The chill of the desert night is already upon them.

Mahmood says, "No more semen jokes in Iraq, my friends. Okay? Bush number one makes cease-fire, but no cease-fire in the semen. Thank you, we are saying, for the low sperm count that is killing them in the wombs of their mothers. Thank you for the depleted uranium in our soil and water."

"It was a stupid joke," says Lucchesi from the back seat. He leans forward and puts his hand on Mahmood's shoulder—Mahmood's shoulder twitches.

"In Baghdad the birds are flying upside down. You must forgive my bitterness. Please. Babies born with holes where the eyes are supposed to be. How do you say? A blessing of disguise? In the zoo, they are feeding the lions carrots. I apologize for my bitterness."

An extended silence.

Ruth says, "So, this customs official is your sister. This is interesting to me."

"A way of speaking in Iraq. We have Iraqi blood together. Not family blood. This is of no interest."

Lucchesi says, "But she didn't say, according to your translation, my brother Mahmood. She said my *youngest* brother. Is that also a manner of speaking in Iraq?"

"Soon, maybe tomorrow, we will have massive sandstorm. Very exciting. In sandstorms, we achieve privacy to think about who we are, and what is of interest, and what is not of interest, in our short time on this wounded earth, my friends."

Suddenly Baghdad—city of two skylines. One, perfectly horizontal, except for the punctuation of minarets and the nippled domes of mosques: this is the Islamic skyline of the picturesque, dirty old Baghdad of souks and inward-looking courtyard houses and the densely packed cellular structures of the traditional medina, a place of half-light and darkness, whose perpetually dampened and shaded streets are but narrow alleyways, where chickens and goats roam freely to forage in the strewn garbage: it is the quarter of Saddam's fierce antimodern heart—the Saddam raised in a mud hut in Tikrit, who does not love the other skyline, the secular one of his creation: jagged with high-cut silhouettes of tissue boxes standing on end: new Baghdad, a perpetual construction zone of wide roads and roaring, undisciplined traffic, modern sanitation, shopping centers, German car dealerships, a subway system and above all (literally) the architectural repetitions that bespeak Saddam's penchant for the International Style. This is the city of Saddam's other heart, that loves godless modernity—the city where, nevertheless, among the double-decker buses, the ceaseless blare of horns, and the sea of taxis, on a divided highway you will see, at any given hour, men with full, jutting beards driving donkey carts heavy with produce, barefooted children, and black-veiled women.

"I have good news for you," Mahmood says, as he turns off the highway. "Change of plans. We do not go to Al-Rashid Hotel of journalists and spies. House of vipers. We are going to very rare house Saddam himself picks for you. House of the true Baghdad. Before Westernizing. Such a house is for you because serious artists do not love the inventions of the West, Saddam is believing, and Mahmood is agreeing."

In clogged traffic, at the edge of the old quarter, a boy of perhaps six or seven approaches the halted Mercedes, presses his forlorn face (such big dark eyes) against the closed window on the front passenger side, and stares up at Ruth Cohen. Stares and does not beg or speak. He's not holding in one hand for her observation some pathetic object, in hopes that this nice tourist will give him something, anything, for it. Instead, he's setting himself before her—he is himself the pathetic object. Ruth looks away. The car cannot move. She struggles to maintain a forward gaze. Does not want to look again. Does not want to remember the child in Havana, but her head turns anyway to the beautiful specter at the window. She tries to open the window, but Mahmood has locked all windows and doors. From the backseat Lucchesi says, "Give him this" and hands her a five-dollar bill. She asks Mahmood to release the lock. Mahmood says, bored, "If you want to do this, you can do this," and releases the lock. The boy steps back. She's thinking, How slight he is. She holds out the money. The boy does not take it. Ruth says, "Please." The boy's heartbreaking face has not changed its expression. He does not reach for the bill. Ruth says, "Please." A man rushes out of the crowd, snatches the bill, cuffs the boy hard, then drags him off by the collar, as the boy glances back, expression unchanged, and they are swallowed by the crowd.

Mahmood says, "Father and son business in the old quarter. The boy, Hassan, is famous."

The car cannot move.

Mahmood says, "Children are useful in Baghdad."

❂

In her cold hands, the photo of Lucchesi with his thumbs in his ears, fingers in the flapping position: doing the donkey. She's recalling the night of his birthday dinner, when he'd demonstrated at some length his repertory of Neapolitan gestures, with special emphasis on the categories of scorn, derision, and stupidity. The lingua franca of Mary Street. Performed, he said, because civility demands it, only when the object of the gesture is not present. "You, Ruth, are a civilized person, and would not, therefore, perform them as I do now, when the object of my gestures is sitting directly across from me." How he'd laughed! She smiles faintly, briefly.

"These are the typical lineaments of the stupid ass, and therefore, in order to denote her, it is enough to imitate them. Ruth, watch! This is you:" *Mouth opened, tip of the tongue on the lower lip, chin hanging, eyes half closed, and without any sign of vivacity or spirit.* (At the cracked mirror, she makes the face. Holds it for a long time.) He laughed so hard he cried. He said, "Too bad I couldn't drool—I'll have to work on it. Tomorrow, your assignment is to shoot me doing one of these, so that when I'm gone for good you'll have a reminder of who I really was, and what fun we used to have, when we were young and carefree." Said on the night of his sixty-fifth, she was fifty-two.

The excited newscaster on Ruth's radio is saying that Saddam Hussein has been captured in a spider hole outside Tikrit—lice-ridden in full, wild man's beard. In his hand, not a revolver, or the requisite deadly tablet, but a copy of *The Old Man and the Sea*, while at maximum volume, on a battery-powered cassette player as Special Forces descend upon him, Sinatra singing "Strangers in the Night."

"*One* thumb in ear, palm and fingers oscillating slowly, is sufficient to indicate the ordinary donkey. Like this, up and down. When two hands are used, like this, like this, we express the superlative degree—*un stupido supremo*. That's us, Ruth, jackasses supreme. Because we live like hermits."

Crunch of dry twigs—under a wintry sun, the hermit walks the border of the blazing lake when a partridge flushes suddenly like whirling thunder beneath her feet and her heart is seized. Is this the end? She leans against a tree, looking waterward, transfixed by the glitter. Violence in the chest. The landscape tilts. Is this, then, the donkey's end? Alone in an idyllic setting, where no human sounds break the silence, too weak to cry out, were there any point in doing so. (*Stupid ass*.) "Nature," he'd said? "Nature is a natural disaster. We should go back to the house on Mary Street. That's where we belong." She sits. A loon passes before her, tilting, near the tilted shore, but here, at Ninth Lake, there are no loons. (He wanted loons to cry in the night, as he lay sleepless in his narrow bed.) She lies in the pine needles, in the fragrance of pine needles. Violence in the chest.

When you are normal, you do not feel it beating. That erratic jumping thing in your chest is the heart out of rhythm, when the blood flow constricts and you grow pale and cold—colder than you've ever been, though wrapped in three layers of winter clothing. Inhale the fragrance, Ruth, and breathe deeply, try to breathe deeply, though you cannot, and think the mantra that Larry taught you: Inhale, *calm*, exhale, *down*. If you die, you may be found in the Spring thaw, as a pile of icy wet bones (how white they are!). Your body? Your body was an extended feast for raccoons, possums, crows, vultures, insects and worms. Your body was.

What had he said in Baghdad? He called himself the metaphysician of Mary Street. If you fall on Mary Street, you won't need to say your mantra more than once. Because Mary Street is where there is life. Mary Street is Utica's old quarter. Where deeds precede words and ideas. Where gestures are words. Where gestures and words cohabit, happily interdependent. Where, when there are no gestures, words are gestural—angular and lined with flesh. The voice on Mary Street is tissue, a single skin binding bodies in communication. Forget the worthless abstractions and embrace, and be embraced, by the sounds of voices. Better to be connected, he'd said in bed, in Baghdad. Listen for the grain of the voice, taste the skin of connection. I learn this about Mary Street in the cafes of the old quarter. She fights the sleep that would seal her up in final rest.

Leaning heavily on a crooked stick, she rises. Walks to the water's edge—to stare, be blinded and consumed by the fire on the lake. Violence in the chest. At the shore, looks back across the inlet to the two faded cabins. Death row, he'd called them on their second day in Baghdad, when she'd spent the late morning and afternoon with Saddam, at his Republican Palace. Picture taking, an elegant lunch, picture taking and conversation about picture taking. The President is intrigued and quite eager, Ruth Cohen, to become acquainted with your philosophy of the camera. Be so kind as to enlighten him.

He wanted to talk only about the sound of Arabic voices. He spent the days in outdoor cafes, in the old quarter, thrilled, how fortunate he felt not to comprehend, he wanted to make that clear to her, how fortunate, not a single word, swept up and absorbed drinking mint tea, smoking the water pipe, *shisha*—he'd drifted, stoned on the mint tea and *shisha*, inhaling the peach-flavored tobacco, and the Arabic voices also inhaled. It was the thrill of something aurally manifest and stubborn, before the meaning of words, in no service of communication. What he heard were sounds unlike any he'd ever heard, delivering to his clueless American ear the pleasures of total opacity. Here, in Baghdad, in the absence of signification, a thing direct, the Arabic speaker's enfleshed voice, channeled to his astonished ear—he was wide open!—from deep in the speaker's cavities, his muscles, his membranes, his cartilages, telling a body without civil identity, in an impersonal voluptuousness of the tongue, the glottis, the teeth, the mucous membrane, the nose. A whole carnal stereophony—eroticism without desire and Lucchesi pulled to the other side, not afraid. Beautiful the amber liquid through the glass cup, the mint leaf afloat, his hands cuddling the hot glass cup, on a chilly day in Baghdad.

Sitting on a stone, the thing still jumping in her chest (*in-*

hale), Ruth puts her thumbs in her ears, fingers and palms flapping slowly (*exhale*), and emits a terrible sound, like the braying of a gut-shot jackass, and it's Father Michael's voice now in her head, saying Shit happens, Miss Cohen. And shit is unredeemable. (Sudden tranquility in the chest.) Father Michael says: A child's death is an abomination of God and an argument for atheism. You want theological explanation? Theology is not one of my tools. This child who died before your eyes. I'll not tell you that you bear no responsibility. You will suffer for that death for as long as you live. For as long as you breathe. Had you not gone to Cuba it wouldn't have happened. The logicians will argue that you are not the cause. But logic is not one of our tools, is it Miss Cohen? We find it empty. Why shut the door on such intimate events? Why even try? I can't relieve you. Wouldn't even if I could. Can't relieve myself ...I spend my afternoons in hospitals, with the dying. We don't talk. We pray. They say, Hold my hand, Father. Then a beautiful nurse appears and I cannot pray, and I want to hold her hand ...Do you believe in God? A stupid question. God may not believe in us...The child died, horribly, before your eyes. Were you a Christian I'd remind you that suffering is the significance of the Cross. Miss Cohen, your suffering is luminous because you suffer for another. Good. Very good! Most do not. Most suffer selfishly, in the dark. You're the latest Jew with a cross—a featured actor in the divine comedy. It may be one day you'll find cause in that to rejoice, though I doubt it. I wouldn't myself. "But was the child's suffering significant of anything but appalling darkness?" It's time, Ms. Cohen, to say goodnight.

(*A dog might be the thing after all. An unstrokable dog.*)

✺

The exhausted foreign curiosities struggle through the al-Gailani souk, rolling suitcases behind them, as Mahmood parts the friendly crush—past the cafes of silent, heavy-lidded men they go; past the butcher shop, whose blood-slick carcasses hang in the open air (the fly-stickers of Old Baghdad); past the vendors of Saddam pencils, Saddam lighters; past the gleaming wares of the coppersmiths and the silversmiths, the aromatic stalls of roasting, marinated chickens and ravishing sweets, the hawkers of Saddam t-shirts, Saddam watches, Saddam posters; through the wash of Arabic and the arresting spectacle of Baghdadis in traditional dress; past the ancient reed weavers and now a startling boy, perhaps fifteen, a transported boy in a Chicago Bulls warm-up outfit, miming jump shot after jump shot. It is Dhafir al-Sayyid, who has no English, but when Lucchesi sings out "Michael Jordan!" he grins the mother of all grins, he forgets his game, forgets the roar of the crowd at Madison Square Garden, and joins the journey.

They turn off the souk into a deserted alley of doorways carved elaborately in geometric patterns—promises of a hidden world of elegance—but Ruth and Lucchesi are punished by a rigid blankness of walls, in a crooked corridor several donkeys wide, bisected with a gutter that runs a dark stream of viscous consistency, where feral cats feed by night. From the rooftops, accomplished fingers pick mournful melodies. The Americans have entered the labyrinth of Baghdad's suffering poor.

Mahmood rattles something rough-toned in Arabic. The boy runs off.

Lucchesi says, "Another of your beautiful and devious beggars?"

Mahmood ignores the question—"Here we are, be happy," and stops at a heavy wooden door, inlaid with ivory and mother-of-pearl, before which stand two impassive guards.

Down the long passageway—a dogleg left, so much the better to keep the eyes of the street from seeing within, and suddenly a gracious courtyard, a fine fountain at its center, with ficus in decorated pots arranged around the periphery. On a low teak table, near the fountain, catching spray, a golden bowl of dates and figs and a pitcher of pomegranate juice. With a gesture taking in the entire expanse of the three-story colonnaded structure Mahmood says, "Your home for five days. Are you happy? I am very happy if you permit Mahmood to read your book for a day, because I have never read such a big American writer." Lucchesi grants the request, immediately, without correcting the characterization.

Then a whirlwind tour—because Mahmood has special business with his son, Dhafir al-Sayyid—through the daunting house of more than two thousand square meters, of one hundred fifteen rooms that vary in size from large domed reception halls on the first floor, with chandeliers in decorated brass, walls covered in ceramic tiles and splendid rugs and a dazzling filigree of joinery, to large and small rooms for living purposes, many of them giving on to the galleried second and third floors, overlooking the courtyard. No views to or from the street—"because Islamic architecture, my friends, is for protecting our secrets. Do you have secrets? Does the camel shit in the desert?" Eight full bathrooms in marble with domes of many-colored glass, molded and painted wooden walls and ceilings everywhere, doors inlaid with glazed metals everywhere, walls of windows of turned wood (floor to ceiling), colored marble mosaic floors, a number of underground tunnels, whose existence Mahmood does not bother to disclose, a maze of stairwells and hallways, arabesques and geometrics of fantastic interlacing complexity, foliate designs, floriated wood carvings, paneling perforated so as to spell out Koranic verses. "Where is the furniture?" "Saddam is despising clutter." "I feel lost and overwhelmed." "Me too." "You are not lost. You are in Baghdad." Lucchesi wants to know if the room with the mirrored ceiling might function as a bedroom and Mahmood replies, "Of course, Saddam is very sexual."

Mahmood explains the major functional division: *diwankhana* and *haram*, male and female spaces. "For privacy of the female, for respect of the female, this is also the message of Islam," then bids them goodnight, telling them that the four refrigerators are full, that the wife of one of the guards is at their disposal for cooking and laundry, "but not, please, for the monkey business of the mirrored ceiling."

Tomorrow, Saddam.

❃

In the examination room, alone and brooding, she awaits the entrance of Larry Shapiro, with whom she's had no appointments for a decade.

What occurred three days ago at Ninth Lake had taught her, to her surprise, that she'd prefer to live a while longer—he might be alive. She prefers not to imagine evidence to the contrary, but she imagines it anyway: The gruesome, amateurish video, available on the world wide web. A letter: Dear Ms. Cohen, It is our solemn duty… in your grief.

She hasn't disrobed and donned the gown, though the nurse, proctologically inclined, insisted, Leave it open at the back. She's come only to make arrangements for a medical procedure, to request that the implantable defibrillator be soon implanted. You can't tie the gown in the back unless you're a contortion artist... It always shows your ass. Is my ass falling? A minor surgery with all the risks spelled out in the brochure, puncture of the lungs, damage to blood vessels of the heart, infection, total failure of the device, massive coronary. Larry, who is not a surgeon, says that minor surgery is surgery performed on someone else. No need to disrobe and don the gown just to have a conversation whose point is, Let's do the defibrillator. It was a provisional decision—not the one to do the procedure, but the one to live.

In the past, before her arrival in Utica, it never embarrassed her when a male doctor examined her in her nakedness. With Larry, it was different. (*Dear Ms. Cohen*) She couldn't be sure, since nothing untoward was ever said, or even hinted. What a thought. Something in the way he responded when she visited—his difficulty in completing sentences, the sudden lapses, mid-sentence, as he reached for what turned out to be an ordinary word, or a medical term that he should have had well in hand. At times, a bit of a stutter. And his persistently averted gaze, that most of all, when he did examine her. In my nakedness. (*We regret to inform you*) Perhaps she was wrong about what those awkwardnesses signified, but she really didn't think so. When he gently slid the gown down off her shoulders to examine her breasts, gently, it wasn't fondling, it was an exam, wasn't it? When the gown fell back over her knees, mid-thigh, as she assumed the position in the stirrups, for the pelvic... She thought he might be harboring—a man many years her junior, married with children, a kind man, a charming man, and a brilliant diagnostician with a mysterious power to make his patients feel healthy, even when they were not. (*Results of DNA analysis... dental records confirm*) They left the clinic with a smile. They believed in him—he was the best medicine. With a profession full of Larry Shapiros the big pharmaceuticals would go broke, she once told him, and he'd blushed. Why did he blush? And what if he *were* harboring? Poor guy. Doctors have feelings too. How do they keep themselves from having that kind of feeling if they're having that kind of feeling? It's not as if they can say, I decide not to. You're seized. You're just seized. As I was, when I met Lucky. (*It is my grievous duty, as Special Assistant to the Secretary of State*) A person is just dragged along. What chance does anyone have against such a feeling? Larry had to look, touch me—what if he feels?—and put his finger... Poor guy. She hopes that she's wrong, but she doesn't think so. Lucky's words, when we landed in Baghdad, were mischievously delivered: "A woman with a past and a man, at seventy-one, looking for a dramatic future." (*I think Lucky's dead.*)

My tits are falling. The sky is falling. This varicose vein. My hearing is going... Whatever fantasies he feeds his heart on, oh the sight of me now—it's been a long time—will cure the good doctor for good, if you can be cured of that. But what if he doesn't want curing? Lucky never said a word. Reacted as if I'd never changed. As if he and I were twenty-five. Always made me feel twenty-five, the way he went at me, but now that he's gone I notice my body—falling everywhere. (*Word out of Iraq: today the remains of American writer Thomas Lucchesi.)*

Larry enters not in standard white coat but in a beautifully cut blue blazer, a smashing sports shirt, stylish tan slacks, and shoes shined to a hard, glossy finish. Why isn't he wearing his white coat? He's prepared, all turned out (for me?) but inside the spiffy ensemble it's still the same old Larry whose behavior tells her what she thinks she'd rather not know.

"Ruth, it's so good to... I mean... I'm sorry for your loss."

"He may not be lost in that sense. We can't be sure... How are you and the family, Larry?"

"Good. Good. Kerry's a junior at Kennedy, I can't believe it, and Kathleen turned two in August. The terrible twos. Good to see you, Ruth."

"Good to see you too."

An uncomfortable pause.

"And your wife?"

"Megan. Good. Megan's good. We're all good. How can I help you?" Fiddling with his ballpoint pen and clipboard.

And if she knew, for sure, that Lucky were dead? Give the good doctor what he wants? Why not? What's the difference? Matters more to them than to us. They think too much of it, about it. Men. Lucky. Larry. Once he sees what he's getting, gotten, if he can actually go through with it, not with his fingers this time in me but with his, in this old lady, the good doctor will be cured for good. Drain off his every drop of fantasy and then when he goes home without his fantasy he can be there full time in his mind, then he'll become real at last, at home, and when he makes love to Megan it will be Megan, the actuality of her flesh and tongue and not some ghostly presence, ghastly me that he's… But if he's not cured by my deteriorating body? I'm leaving my wife and kids because I… What a horror. No, I wouldn't do it. Why would I want to again if Lucky? From the grave, if that's where he is, he'd haunt me. See, I told you you would betray me when I'm dead. I want my husband back. Where is he?

"It's settled, then, good," he's saying, "I'll arrange everything at St. Elizabeth's. It's an outpatient thing, three-four hours tops, a follow-up three days later, then another one in about ten days, and that's pretty much it. I'm glad you've made this decision, Ruth. Because you're young and you're still –"

"No I'm not, but thank you anyway. Speaking of St. Elizabeth's, I visited Charley DiStefano in the nursing home across the street."

"Did he know who you were?"

"His eyes grew wide when I approached him. He was slumped in his wheelchair. He didn't talk. I said, Nice to see you again, Uncle Charley, and his eyes grew even wider."

"He hasn't walked, rarely speaks, since the stroke. I get reports from my colleague, Corinne DiMarco. She'd make a good doctor for you if you'd like to make a change, I wouldn't take it personally."

(I was wrong. Or he's gotten over it. Or he's testing the water. Or he wants to get over it. Am I disappointed? Why should I be?)

"He spoke to me, Larry. Ten or fifteen minutes after I said Nice to see you again, Uncle Charley, he lifted his head. I hardly recognized him. He said, Nice to see you too, dear. I said, Are you in pain? He replied, It doesn't tickle. His voice was almost familiar. He looked terrible. Skin and bones."

"How long did you stay?"

"About an hour and a half. Just before I left he said, I can't be expected. I touched his hand and he said again, I can't be expected. I said, We can't be expected. Nobody can. When I left I noticed an odor."

"He probably hasn't had control of his bodily functions since the stroke. What? Ten years ago? They change their diapers several times daily. It's an excellent facility."

"Lucky feared that."

"Who?"

"My husband. Feared that might happen to him at the end. Said, if it did, I should shoot him. He may never have to deal with that fear. A consolation, I suppose. I think they murdered him. Of course, if he's really gone he's nothing and the consolation, such as it is, is mine."

"I hope he comes back to you soon."

"I think they murdered my husband... Is Father Michael still at St. Anthony? But why would you keep tabs on a Catholic priest?"

They smile: a welcome change of subject.

Larry says, "No, I don't, but I've read about him in the paper lately. No no. Not that. He was in trouble with the law for another reason. It seems that Father Truck, that's what they're calling him, shows up every Wednesday and Thursday mornings in a run down area, carting in his pick-up paint, ladders, scaffolding, brushes, the whole nine yards. He knocks on a door and offers his services. Free of charge, of course. Exteriors, interiors, whatever they want."

"Charity is now illegal?"

"Taking after the reporter and the camera man with a hammer is. Oh, not on their persons. Their equipment. To smithereens. They only wanted the story, they said. He is said to have said, raising the hammer, This is the story. When he goes before the judge he says, according to the news reports, Your honor, the glamour of publicity is the devil's own medium in our time. I have no regrets, with all due respect to this court, and shall do it again if they insist on publicizing my work. The judge throws out the case and when the assistant D.A. objects the judge replies that he's inclined to report him to the Bar for bringing such frivolity to his courtroom."

"Father Michael was absolved? This is unrealistic. You're making this up."

"Ruth, you forget. This is Utica. The judge is one of his parishioners. So is the assistant D.A. As a result of the news story, and *that* publicity, such is the irony of the Almighty, twenty-seven retirees volunteered their services and now Father Michael has his very own urban renewal crew. Rumor has it that a number of young Latino toughs, who call themselves the Sodality of the Claw Hammer, guard the perimeter of his jobs, ready to dissuade the media in the style of Father Michael."

(She's thinking, He told the story so fluently, with such ease. No lapses. No stuttering. No blushing. He's clearly over it, if he ever had it in the first place.)

"Ruth, I want to ask you something. I may be out of line. If I am, please forgive me."

(*Here we go.*)

"Yes?"

"I was... I mean I *am* fond of Thomas, but... and think about him often... I wonder if you'd mind telling me what he was like in Baghdad. Was he happy? I need a happy image of him in Baghdad. This is childish and totally unprofessional, but I feel that I'm more than a physician to you and Thomas. I need a happy image. Do you have one?"

"Even if I have to lie?"

"Yes."

"I'd like to tell somebody, and who do I know aside from you? I don't mean that the way it sounds. You mean a great deal to the both of us."

"Thank you for saying so. You mean a great deal to me too. The both of you, I mean."

"Larry, I don't have to tell you a benign lie. He was happy. He really was. He was absorbing the life of a culture utterly foreign to our experience. He would have said *it* was absorbing *him*, and that's why he'd come back at dinnertime like a large child who's finally gotten what he wants. How's that for the happy image you requested?"

"Perfect."

"It's true. And he was writing again, he told me."

"About Baghdad."

"About Utica. East Utica. Mary Street. He said that Baghdad gave him the desire to write about life rooted in a place. Organic culture is how he put it. He was finally going to write his Utica novel, and do it right. Organic fiction. He'd finally cast aside the old lacerating need to write a political book worthy of *Cuban Stories*. He believed Baghdad would make him a political artist.

But Baghdad had the opposite effect. He thought we should move back to Mary Street. He was very happy."

"He was fulfilled."

"Yes."

"A lucky man. Who gets to be fulfilled?"

"Fulfillment with a bad ending."

"And you came home to all that disturbing publicity. CNN and the *Times*. They came here trying to find you. The tabloids. Return of The Scarlet Photographer. We sent them all to Old Forge. How did you manage to avoid the paparazzi?"

"I greeted them all with my shotgun."

"Father Michael would have been proud of you. You said no to the devil."

"Give my best to your wife."

"I shall."

"Give her yours, too, doctor."

"As often as I can, Ruth."

❇

She had anticipated the excesses of marble and gold at the Republican Palace on the western edge of the Tigris, but not the simplicity of this underlit room into which she is ushered, with its great windows open to the river, bone white walls adorned with no pictures, no rugs, nothing at all; a floor of rough-textured concrete, painted black; a long table of inexpensive wood (parson's style, she thinks, noting with an inner smile the cultural irony of the analogy), finished in clear lacquer—barren except for a pitcher of ice water and three glasses; and a ceiling of gracious height, also in black.

He's seated behind the table, at the center, his broad back to the brown-rushing river. The translator, Habib Aziz, is seated at the far end. They rise in unison. Habib is a short, thin man, forgettable in traditional robe, headdress, and sandals, a recent graduate of Oxford, M. Phil., whereas (the contrast has been arranged) the Leader cuts a blazing figure—tall and powerfully built, impeccably groomed and subtly cologned in a silk pin stripe suit, custom tailored in London, with a maroon handkerchief of white striping fluffed a little outrageously in his breast pocket: a touch of the old reprobate, the secret decadent, in this ascetic space of his design. Such luxuriant wavy hair—very good looking by any standard, Ruth thinks. An opinion she'll not pass on to her husband, and one she wishes she hadn't had.

The translator stands at the table as Saddam ("the one who confronts") comes forward to greet her. She puts out her hand and he takes it in both of his, with a slight bow of the head, speaking in Arabic with lyrical intonation. The translator says, "The President wishes you to know that your pleasure is his. That you have only to speak your pleasure, Ruth Cohen, and it shall be granted."

She loads her camera, saying, "This"—holding up the camera—"is my pleasure." Habib translates for Saddam, Saddam replies, and Habib translates for Ruth: "The President admires the commitment of a serious artist. He is himself a writer who has published three novels." Saddam taps the table with his pen and speaks. Habib translates: "Forgive me, three fictions in the classic mode of romance. Not novels. As an Oxford graduate I should know this generic distinction. It is conceivable that I am not my father's son, the President is saying."

Saddam comports himself with this foreign guest as he has comported himself with no other. When he addresses her, he does not look at the translator, as is his wont, or at the pen turning constantly in his hands. He looks at her directly, never averting his gaze, and speaks with rare animation, with no trace of his typically phlegmatic, virtually thick-tongued manner—as if they shared the language, and so much else. She will find him charming and warm and feel the frightening urge to trust him. How difficult he makes it to credit the reports of a butcher who sanctions torture and mass killing, who himself had done murder when young, and when not so young—without emotion, they said, no rage, in ice cold will.

She will try to keep herself from thinking that he is easy to like, but she will fail. She will remember (to little avail) that persons of fame and power, in person, obliterate all the horrific reports, by sheer shattering presence. That they are, like erotic fantasies, virtually beyond resistance.

An aide appears with a third chair. Saddam gestures for her to sit. The camera is slung sexily around her neck. She places her tripod bag on the floor next to the chair—on the chair itself her large camera bag bearing extra batteries, two back up camera bodies, a portrait lens, a flash unit, twenty rolls of thirty-six exposures each, and the inscribed copy of *The Prostate Dialogues*, returned by Mahmood that morning. She'll have no use for the tripod, the flash unit or the portrait lens. This will be intimate and candid work, of hundreds of shots, mostly of the head and upper torso.

She says, "Thank you. I have come to work, not to sit and converse." Saddam smiles; Saddam likes Ruth.

He speaks in a tone that says, "Of course, we agree, how could we not?" Habib translates: "The President asserts that in good company we may both work and converse. Are you sympathetic?" Before she can reply Saddam speaks harshly to Habib, who corrects himself: "The President does not assert, he *suggests*, that in good company we may work and converse *hand in hand*. Are you sympathetic?"

She realizes that Saddam understands English perfectly—and likely speaks it fluently. Nevertheless, she'll not trim her words. She replies, "Inform Mr. Hussein that my camera has a built in light meter which requires that I approach him frequently. To place it within a few inches of his moustache."

Saddam is pleased. Unlike Ruth Cohen, the Leica M6 will prove to be adequate to the challenges of its subject.

Habib says, "The President wishes to convey that he has no fear. The President is asking, Do you? He requests I tell you that in the village in which he was raised, conversing is considered equivalent to playing. To have conversation with good company is to have the most intimate of pleasures. And in such pleasure, the poor of his village are as blessed as the wealthy of Baghdad. Feel free, he says, to approach frequently."

As she approaches, Saddam turns in his chair and gestures toward the windows and speaks softly and briefly. "The President says that the river is a strong brown god." Saddam, again briefly. "The river is untamed and intractable." Saddam nodding now, speaking at greater length. "The brown god is forgotten, unpropitiated and dishonored by the dwellers of this great city, but not by the people of his village, whom it destroys in its implacable rages." Saddam turns back in his chair to Ruth, speaking as she shoots him close, hovering over the brooding philosopher. "As a youth I swam often in the river, and now the river is inside me. I do not know much about the brown god, I do not know what it means, only that its rhythm pulses in my blood and that I would write sentences like the waves on the river, because then, truly, I would be a writer of force."

(Lucchesi, the prey, strolling aimlessly in the old quarter, followed at a discreet distance by Dhafir al-Sayyid, whose father, Mahmood, had lectured him sternly the night before on his repeated acts of truancy. They reach a crowded square, where the boy makes a wide half-circle, then turns and bears directly down on Lucchesi, who does not notice. When he's within five feet, Dhafir shouts Michael Jordan! Lucchesi, without Arabic, grateful for a companion, bows a deep theatrical bow and gestures for the truant-without-English to join him.)

Saddam unbuttons his jacket, sits back and spreads his knees, revealing crotch and belt buckle, with an inscription in Arabic. Because when you fight the Great Satan you must fight satanically. Consequently, he had instructed Habib to do research on American poses, and Habib had shown him Banana Republic advertisements in *The New York Times Magazine*.

Ruth snaps numerous full body shots, as she slowly circles the subject. As if reading her mind, Habib says, "The inscription signifies, This is Saddam's belt." Saddam says something and laughs.

Habib says, "He wishes to add what is not on the belt, just for you, a very special guest: Abandon all hope, ye who venture below."

She goes to the camera bag to withdraw Lucchesi's novel. Saddam follows. She gives him the book. He holds it, front jacket facing her, as she snaps shot after shot. (One year later, the photo will adorn the front jacket cover of the Knopf reprint.) He asks Habib to translate Lucchesi's inscription ("Struggle against chronic illness is fatal"). Saddam speaks with sudden gravity. Habib translates: "Iraq is America's chronic illness and Little Bush struggles fatally, like Big Bush, with the failure of his leadership."

(They walk in silence toward a park and a soccer field by the river, Lucchesi in Dhafir's tow, thinking, This is what it must be like to be the father of a son, and Dhafir pointing at that very moment to Lucchesi, saying, "Abu Dhafir" (father of Dhafir), which Lucchesi does not, of course, understand. Lucchesi thinking, This is what it must be like to be the father of a teenage son. You don't understand one another. You don't speak the same language. And yet you wish to be close to one another, though you don't know how to communicate such a thought—it is too embarrassing. So you walk together in intimate and painful silence. And many years later, when you are separated by geographical or emotional distance, or both, likely both, or by the death of your son, or your father, you remember that day of the walk to the park by the river, when you could not say to him the things that you wanted to say, and never in your life said.)

For Habib's second assignment in the satanic lore of American poses, Saddam had directed him to acquire photo books of JFK, so that Saddam could enact for *The New Yorker* certain Oval Office pictures of Kennedy, long burned into American memory. The one where he's standing back to camera at the front of the desk, leaning stiff-armed on the desk, head tilted down, hunched over, as if reading. Directly behind the desk, a large window, so that, backlit, JFK is a darkened figure of concentration, a great man focused on the work of his people, though I truly do not believe, Saddam thought, that he was reading, or even much thinking. I believe that in this picture Kennedy was doing what I so often do. Mourning his loneliness. Or the profile shot at the window in silhouette, in the most familiar of his postures: hand in jacket pocket, elbow jutted out. What was he thinking? Nothing. He was posing in America. Kennedy was less than his pictures. That was why they killed him. We have the picture. The person is totally disappointing. Kill him, oblige him with death, because he does not wish to be less than his picture. In my village, we care not for pictures. In a mosque, no images. I have permitted many of myself, like an infidel, who with these pictures of himself for America wishes to subvert the infidels with images that say, Behold the man, Saddam Hussein! A person very like you. Am I less than my picture? No doubt.

So many conspiracies, so few to trust. Perhaps they will kill me too. I have killed so many who wish with complete malignancy to kill me, but I have not yet killed everyone who wishes to kill me. After all, one cannot kill everyone, not even in Iraq—so broods Saddam, as Ruth, who knew the Kennedy pictures well, shoots him many times as JFK.

Let me be fortunate with this woman as Kennedy, they say,

was fortunate with her—he, who like me, was fortunate with so many. She is not young, but is thrilling still and it would be thrilling to be with her, God willing, who was with the enormous American myth.

Like Kennedy, I will be destroyed. The great Hemingway teaches that a true man will always be destroyed, but never defeated. I, Saddam Hussein, was not born for defeat, God willing.

(No prostate medication for two days and he's feeling the effects: slow, painful, and meager urination every thirty minutes, and now, on the streets of Baghdad with this boy, what can he do? The cafes offer no rest rooms. The restaurants are closed and no public facilities in sight. How can he indicate his problem to the boy without making in gesture what could only be taken as an untoward suggestion? Twice he finds an alley, gestures for the boy to wait, follows it behind a building and relieves himself, like a dog, against a garbage bin in the first instance and a moribund date palm in the second. When they reach the park, he needs to once again and disappears into a vast thicket of bamboo.

Thanks to his cunning decision at breakfast to take no fluids, with the exception of a single large glass of juice, and thanks to the rigors of a long brisk walk on which he'd worked up a splendid sweat, he finds himself, as he emerges from the thicket, at last symptomless, truly relieved, and a little light-headed. He's suffering from first stage dehydration, though he doesn't yet know it, as he and the boy meet at the soccer field two other truants of Dhafir's acquaintance and choose sides: it's Lucchesi and the two new boys versus Dhafir, the Pelé of Baghdad, as he's known at school. Like his team, Lucchesi will soon find himself in serious trouble.)

An aide in chef's hat and apron wheels in a serving cart. He's about to set places for lunch when Saddam says something to him, causing the aide to turn and leave, but when he reaches the door Saddam again speaks, and the aide returns, removes his hat and apron and gives them to Saddam, who promptly dons hat and apron, wheels the cart to the table, sets the places, picks up the soup ladle and has an idea. Habib tells Ruth, "He wishes for you to take his picture." Ruth tries, but fails to hide her amusement. Saddam has caused her to smile and Saddam is happy. She snaps Chef Hussein's photo many times. One of these becomes the opener in *The New Yorker* photo essay.

He begins to serve. As he ladles the soup into Ruth's bowl he has another idea, which he communicates to Habib, who says, "The President would be greatly honored if you would make it possible for me to take your picture with him, as he serves you." She says, "Brilliant," and instructs Habib, who snaps several photos of the grinning Chef and his guest. When he's finished serving the lentil soup, the lamb on a bed of dill rice, the sides of yogurt and mixed pickles, he sits to partake with his guest, having removed the apron but not the hat—eager to discuss Ruth's philosophy of photography, while softly in the background, piped through speakers artfully hidden in the four walls—Sinatra, "It Had to be You." Habib says, "Saddam loves Frank Sinatra." Saddam replies and Habib says, "But not Bing Crosby. Nix on *der Bingle*!"

The time is propitious, as he guesses. Intimacy with this woman is his destiny. In English, he dismisses Habib. She does not give him the satisfaction of a surprised reaction.

"What I intend," she says, trying but failing to avert her gaze, "as a photographer, never comes out as I intend it."

"What I intend," he toasts her, "always comes out as I intend it."

"I stand in front of something, instead of arranging it. I arrange myself."

"I have always found it a pleasure to arrange others."

"Geometry is the supreme pleasure, the corroboration of absolute structure. I desire that geometric values be the end of my art, but I have failed to achieve my end."

"You do not desire to represent the stories of individuals in your art?"

"I do not desire to represent anything."

"Then we agree completely. It is torture to represent individuals, and I prefer not to be tortured. Better to give than to receive."

"The stories of individuals cause pain."

"To you?"

"Yes."

"Better to give than to receive."

She's not touched her food.

"I would make a photograph as an altogether new object, complete and self-contained, whose basic condition is order, inside the independent world of the photograph."

"Unlike," Saddam replies, with sudden intensity, mouth full, spitting particles, "the actual world of events and actions, whose permanent condition is change and disorder and ugliness."

"Yes."

"We are in complete sympathy, Ruth Cohen."

"But I have failed to achieve my artistic desire."

"I do not fail," cutting into his lamb.

"In your fiction?"

"Fiction is my minor art."

"What is your major art?"

"I think of myself as the artist-President, who sculpts his raw material, the Iraqi people, into the condition of absolute structure, free of the disorders of change. Ruth Cohen, how do you like my hat? Do I amuse you? Do you think that I am a clown?"

Sinatra: "I've Got You Under My Skin."

Ruth thinks, This is terrible. This is truly terrible. I feel no fear. No revulsion. None whatsoever, in the presence of this monster.

(He's pale, faint and cold. He vomits. Frightened, the two truants they'd met at the field run off. Lucchesi says to Dhafir, "Did the Yankees win?" Dhafir races to a nearby vendor, who gives him (free of charge) two large bottles of water. When Dhafir returns, he finds a man in a black leather jacket, kneeling at Lucchesi's side. It is his father, who'd come to the park when he learned at Dhafir's school that his son was absent again. Dhafir attempts to remove Lucchesi's backpack but Mahmood, boiling in irritation over his son's truancy, takes it roughly from him, saying there's no chance in hell that Dhafir will receive an actual basketball for his birthday. Mahmood covers Lucchesi with his jacket and Dhafir administers small doses of water (thirty-two ounces) for forty-five minutes, at the end of which Lucchesi has recovered his color, his lucidity, and his need to pee. Dhafir and Mahmood, arms around him, assist him to his feet and to the edge of the thicket, where Mahmood orders his son to stay put for no reason other than a repeatedly defied father's need to assert the fantasy of his authority. They enter the thicket. When they come out, Lucchesi is smiling, saying, "The pause that refreshes." Mahmood gives Dhafir money to purchase lunch, but the vendor refuses payment, reminding the boy of the beautiful practice of Arab hospitality, particularly when a foreigner is in need, even if the foreigner is an American.

Directly across the river, some five hundred yards away—at the Republican Palace, where Ruth and Saddam discuss the virtues of nonrepresentational art and politics—a surveillance team, responsible for security at the park along the Tigris, prepares a report, for Saddam's eyes only, on the behavior of Special Agent Mahmood al-Sayyid and the husband of the American photographer.)

She stands on the table, at the end of a long afternoon. He sits with his back to her, looking directly at the ceiling. She shoots down on his face: Saddam inverted. He leans forward in his chair, right elbow propped on knee, hand up, fingers spread wide: staring at his palm as she shoots lying on the floor. Then, within a foot of Saddam—his eyes, his glittering eyes. Finally, with three exposures left in the last roll, a use for the flash unit: classic mug shots in harsh light.

He rises and approaches with a bold stare. She says, "As a photographer I learned that nothing you plan will ever come to life."

"And that is precisely why I always plan with the utmost care. My fair lady, stay the evening and we shall dine and discuss the sad failure of *Godfather III*."

"Goodbye, Mr. President—I loved that movie."

She imagines Lucchesi on the platform, snapping photo after photo of The Mad Woman of Ninth Lake. She's naked, white-bodied, a ghost pulling over ice and snow the cracked, free-standing mirror, when she slips and falls hard, clinging to the mirror as it comes shattering down upon her in a thousand shards. (Good. Smash all cameras too.) Blood on the snow. (Good.)

Quick! Arise and dance naked for the missing man. Resurrect him with salacious gyrations. For once, make yourself a clown— as he had on so many occasions made himself a clown for you, to retrieve you from your brooding remoteness.

Look! How he leaps in desire! (Whose desire?) Here he comes, all the way back on this bitter day—past all difficulty leaping, convulsed in laughter he leaps past death itself. (Is my husband dead?)

When will you dance?

She bleeds from several small cuts on her hands and one on her inner thigh. (Where he lingered.) Scoops snow in both hands and presses it against her breasts. (Where he sucked. But no babes sucked.) Rises and retreats to the cabin, to put on his robe, tend to her wounds, stoke the dying fire. Or maybe not. (Quick! Go out and finish the job. Your first work of performance art: The Abominable Snow Woman.)

I wonder if there's any hot chocolate? (He would have said.) Because these, Ruth, are the halcyon days of hot chocolate and hot sex. Maybe someone will make me a cup of hot chocolate, not because I'm incapable of doing it for myself, but because it tastes so much better when you do it for me. Piping hot, on this terrible day. Put a little whipped cream on top and I'll return the favor, I'll whip up concupiscent curds, just for you. I feel today as if in my great good luck I'd married a nurse. Or a girl just like the girl who married dear old dad. (Dead. Unnursed.)

Shuffling about the cabin in his slippers, sipping hot chocolate. (This is his blood.) Pauses, long, opposite the place on the wall where the big fork he'd thrown that time had struck and gouged. Touches the gouged place. (I do this in memory of you.)

A bath, as hot as she can bear it, lowering herself weeping into the tub, remembering again, how many times? The wailing boy who came to their door in Baghdad on the morning of departure, as they awaited Mahmood and the ride to the airport. The boy hand in hand with a man who identified himself as the boy's teacher. The boy crying a river of Arabic, a torrent of tears like rain drops on his shoes—she sees the dampened shoes again and the teacher translating and Lucchesi saying Wait, wait. This is the boy who helped me in the park. This is Mahmood's son. And the teacher saying, Boy is needing very big. Boy is weeping, because Mahmood is arrested in the bed of Magda al-Radi. Boy is saying where is my father? Please, Abu Dhafir—calling you Father of Dhafir because too much pain of needing where is my father, I have no mother, beseeching you and kind lady. They have shot Magda al-Radi. Who is Magda al-Radi? I am lacking, Abu Dhafir help me. They are killing, why are they killing? Kind lady are you saving my father? Sir, be taking Dhafir to Saddam to save true father... Abu Dhafir Abu Dhafir... Thank you... You are beseeching Saddam, please. Thank you. Kind lady, are you beseeching? Are you sad?

Lies back in the steaming bath, wanting to smoke again, wanting to drink too much, wanting to sleep all day and all night in the hot bath of her last pleasure, reviewing like the phrase of a song in her mind that repeats relentlessly, it drives her to the edge, this fantasy of heroic Ruth, the fantasy of somehow—in the chaos of the American occupation, somehow getting into Iraq, overland from Jordan, stowed away in a truck hauling produce for Baghdad and somehow finding the boy whose given name she's forgotten. Do you know any families without a father named al-Sayyid? Oh yes, kind lady, a thousand. Somehow bringing the boy forlorn, taking him back to Utica and 1311 Mary Street, my adopted son whose name is somehow. Somehow, forgive me for your father's death and for your sister's in Havana before you, raising him forlorn and happy in America, without the American father, the Abu who disappeared in his broken country—without the orange and brown afghan his mother made for him sixty years ago. No medications. No hot chocolate. Seventy-one years old. With just a pen and in his back pocket—her final sight of him—as he walked away and turned to say his last words—he would have called it his exit line—patting the notepad in his back pocket, "To catch the last forced trickle of my creative energy. As a man pees, so does he write." No goodbye because why would he? Had she smiled? Did he? She can't remember. Did she say hurry back? Ruth, he would have said, if he knew—it would have been just like him to have said it, "This is a culture for which I can well imagine losing my head." (Whose witticism?) Larry, I'd like you to meet my Iraqi son, whose name I've forgotten, and my Cuban daughter, whose name I never knew.

The mind is its own place—how he loved to quote the classic poets, the dark ones, especially those in their darkest moments. They made him happy. Try laughing, he said. Try the black-hearted poets for comedy. Myself am hell. You too, Ruth, laughing.

Turns on the hot water spigot, slides down deeper in the tub, submerged to the chin—my severed head afloat. The terror of the dark, he said joyfully at breakfast. He'd been awake since 4:00. Sleep badly with me and await the vanquishment of the dark, when the voice at dawn calls to prayer. Come, come, prayer is better than sleep! Pray with me! There is no God but Allah and Mohammed is his prophet. Surrender, surrender! Islam is surrender!

What have we surrendered, Ruth? What have we given in our separate cabins, where the spider weaves our last will and testament? Do we know any of God's ninety-nine names?

Come, come to the mosque—sings the voice from the minaret—all who hear come and praise God. A tower beside a mosque. For vocal projection. In honor of the voice. (He was so eager, a schoolboy bringing home his lessons.) The al-Gailani mosque, he said, and a school, a public bath, a public fountain, a souk. In all these places they gather. With whom have we gathered? In the vicinity of the voice, whose aural reach defines the neighborhood, they gather. Nearness is all. What voice have we heard at Ninth Lake? (Nearer, my God, to nobody.) The voice in long arching and aching lines—the breath control! The fluidity! A river of sound traversing the registers of lamentation and ecstasy, I cannot tell the difference, winding down the streets and alleys—saturating the public square, curling about the houses and cafes, commandeering the souk, lingering over the rooftops, waking the goats and turkeys, soothing the dogs who will not howl, rubbing its sinuous phrases against the window panes, licking its tones into the corners of resistant night, and night falters, as the voice drinks the dark down to the dregs.

He'd asked Mahmood, What is the precise moment of dawn? How is it determined? And Mahmood told him that the singer in the tower holds up before him in the pitch of night a single black thread—its visibility is dawn, and the launch of his voice.

He wanted to test Mahmood's story. The next day at 4:00 a.m. Could I provide a thread? Would I listen with him? Be swept up with him? I don't like to be alone, Ruth.

She'd never seen him like that. The floating head smiles a little, remembering how beside himself he'd been that morning. He'd put himself aside. He'd surrendered.

There is a voice, Mahmood had told him, from the other side of the Tigris. Unamplified. Some say it is true. Winding across wide water. Nonsense, others are saying. Allah akbar! You could hear it at dawn, even from this side of the Tigris, if you were devout. So many of us are not. I am not. If you had truly vanished into God. So many of us desire the things of the West. I do not hear the voice. Are you wishing to hear as a devout Muslim? Are you needing to disappear? I am thinking that Ruth Cohen desires it more. (Put ourselves aside. What Lucky wanted for us. Together to relinquish the selves of our isolation.)

She takes a deep breath and goes under, but cannot stay under long enough.

Comes up gasping, remembering the night in Baghdad, when

he said, We've made love in the harem. We're horny infidels. Tonight we violate the oldest unwritten law of this culture—the code of social restraint that Saddam violated by building this three-story extravaganza in the midst of two-story houses, which used to be the limit when Baghdad was entirely an old quarter, when they respected the privacy of the family without exception. (Professor Lucchesi.) Before the exception of Saddam, whose philosophy is, Your privacy is my business, because in your privacy you hatch plans for my death. Better you than me. Did he make a move on you, Ruth? (You'll never tell the truth, or I'll never believe your response, so don't bother answering.) In the long hot summer these people take to the roofs in the evening. On a mild night like tonight they'll be out there. The high roof walls make it impossible for one family to spy on another. Thanks to Saddam we can survey old Baghdadi life in its hidden authenticity. We'll see, but not be seen. And when we've sated ourselves with feasts of the eye, we'll do something on the roof, which is why I'm bringing these three blankets. To cushion our ancient bones. One more for the road. Because we're not quite sated.

As she gazed, she lost herself, dissolved into the objects and scenes of her contemplation—she was filled to the brim with the roof life all around them: A man writing by candlelight. A woman watching television. A boy and a girl kicking a soccer ball, practicing headers. The ball flying over the parapet. Meat on a grill over an open fire. Flamboyantly colored undergarments, fluttering on a clothesline hung between the chicken coop and the pigeon coop. A tethered goat. A teenage girl gazing at the moon—

a boy gazing at the girl. An old woman ironing. Six people seated around a low table, a few inches off the floor, eating. Men at board games. A Coke sign, circa 1955. A flower garden. An herb garden. In the corners, the jumbled debris piles—pieces of pipe, broken ceramic tiles, a door, scrap lumber, scrap sheet metal, broken glass. In the far distance, many open fires. Many satellite dishes.

Pathetic what I retain: a dead list, a mechanical enumeration of objects, but the life swirling on those roofs, swirling even in the debris piles and the outright garbage, where has it gone? The life that swirled me that night. Where is it? Gestures, odors, voices. The gaiety and the solemnity. Cannot call it up, has left no residue.

Who am I? A mind of winter. I've been cold a long time. No difference now between the memories of that night and those of the reception hall at Heathrow, on the return trip. All stale and inert—like a series of photographs. Chocolate Box, Sunglass Hut, Chanel, Burberry, Bureau de Change, Rolex, 24-Hour Cash, 24-Hour Money.

In the distance we could see the al-Gailani Mosque, named for a legendary mystic. There, once a week, the dervishes whirl out to God. In ecstasy, they put themselves aside.

She opens the cabin door and steps naked into the mean wind, the slanting snowstorm, and begins to whirl.

✦

FOR: LEADER-PRESIDENT

CONCERNING: Surveillance via telephoto photography of activities of Special Agent Mahmood al-Sayyid and the American Thomas Lucchesi husband of American photographer Ruth Cohen 24 October 2002 at Freedom Fields Park during photographic session of Leader-President and American photographer.

MOST HONORED SIR: Between approximately twelve hundred and thirteen hundred hours in company of a child (male) since determined to be child of Agent al-Sayyid, American Lucchesi (presumed novelist) theoretically collapsed on soccer field of Freedom Fields Park (photo #1). Following said collapse child brought water to administer to American when Agent al-Sayyid arrived suddenly running toward American and child (photo #2). Child removed backpack from fallen American (photo #3) and al-Sayyid with swiftness tore backpack from child (photo #4). After forty-five minutes of water administration al-Sayyid with backpack in left hand (photo #5) and American and child proceed toward thicket of bamboo. At thicket al-Sayyid makes strong gesture toward child (photo #6) and child remains alone at edge of thicket as two adult males disappear into thicket with right arm of al-Sayyid around waist of American while left hand of al-Sayyid holds backpack (photo #7). When adult males emerge from thicket five minutes later (photo #8) backpack is restored to back of American who is smiling broadly (photo #9) as he zips fly (photos #10-20). Agent al-Sayyid also smiles upon emergence (photo #21). Observe that jacket of al-Sayyid bulges at large left side pocket (photo #22). Al-Sayyid holds arm of American as lady holds arm of gentleman of intimacy in the West (photo #23).

CONCLUSION: That an act of treasonous criminality concerning backpack contents took place at Freedom Fields Park in thicket of bamboo where treasonous acts of exchange have occurred in the past. In addition we are confident that acts of unnaturalness took place in thicket between al-Sayyid and American. Consider, Sir, if you will, the smiling upon emergence of the two degenerates. Consider that in all English-speaking societies the vocation of homosexuality and the vocation of espionage are totally unified vocations.

RECOMMENDATION: ABU GHRAIB

❂

He wished to propose something delightful for their last night in Baghdad. If they might possibly be intrigued, then he, Mahmood, would arrange a visit to the home of Magda al-Radi, his former college mate, who had made a niche for herself in the rarefied circles of antiquities restoration.

"I am thinking late afternoon tea, the most exquisite pastries, a balcony with a sweeping view of the river, and a woman who has thoughts completely unknown to the journalists of your country and mine. A serious woman. Yes? Mahmood is thinking that you are already enchanted."

An agent of Saddam's secret service, who proposes a meeting with a woman whose point of view lay outside official opinion? Is that what he'd suggested? Iraqi journalism was Saddam's tool, nothing more. Ruth and Lucchesi knew this. Lucchesi was sure that he recognized the plot from the one espionage novel he'd read. Mahmood a double agent? Something will be given to us by this woman, a Saddam watch—a present to be mailed to a so-called old friend, at an address in Langley, Virginia. Because you cannot mail to America. Thank you so much. Thank you. Their lives were being drawn inside the devious discipline of forbidden fiction.

"No," Ruth replied, "our lives are plotless, and as a consequence virtually unreadable. Too late, Lucky, for melodramatic revision. This will add up to nothing but another disconnected episode. Let's value it for whatever savor it may offer. Why not? A last fling in Baghdad."

At university, Mahmood had nicknamed Magda The Lady of Surprises. He felt (without a trace of evidence) that it touched her essence, whose essence had yet to be touched, whose narrow student life was conducted as a romance of ideas, deep in the bowels of the library's rare book collection—*she*, The Lady of Surprises? How thrilling the thought! It gave her a new sense of self. But was it true? Had she surprised *him*? Quickly, of course, she developed a painful crush on the handsome Mahmood, who liked her, very much, but could not, despite her wealth and intelligence, feel what he suspected she felt. Nevertheless, he treated her with unstinting kindness—which only devastated her all the more. (Haven't seen him in years. Now this phone call and I'm on fire again.)

The first glimpse is unprepossessing: a two-storey house of plain plaster walls, bisected on the first floor by a green door and broken on both levels by green-shuttered windows. (In this brown, desiccated land, she will tell them, green is the color of desire.) No balcony with a sweeping view. There was no balcony. Out front, alongside the path to the house, like an ironic postmodern sculpture, a junk heap of an automobile, paintless, windowless, tireless, and rusted over every square inch, down to the metal.

Mahmood's gleaming Mercedes is met and surrounded by twelve snarling German shepherds. A woman appears. She whistles. The dogs wag their tails and sit. She comes down to greet them. Mahmood is shocked. Tall, six foot one, Mahmood's age (forty-eight), with a build exactly like Rita Hayworth's in her prime, whose signed photo hangs in the foyer. This is not the Magda that he remembers. The height, yes, but always a pathetic sloucher, ashamed of towering (then so plumpishly) over her acquaintances (one could not call them friends), especially the males—especially Mahmood who stood at five foot ten. Who was this trim, statuesque goddess without spectacles? With a flower tucked behind her ear? With such a bold gait and the eyes—the eyes that he remembered as ill-proportioned, too big for the face, now striking him as exotic. Magda al-Radi is suddenly beautiful.

She says, "Mahmood," offering her hand, which he takes in both of his, his jaw a little dropped—too surprised, he'd tell her later that night, when he'd returned, to respond. (You are truly The Lady of Surprises, he'd said. And she considered, then quickly dismissed the implicit comparison. She thought herself a realist.) Mahmood too flustered even to introduce the guests until she prompted him. She thinks, He is not the man he used to be. A little potbelly now, dark circles and a heaviness beneath the eyes, they no longer sparkle. He looks tired. The kind of tired that cannot be alleviated. Yet he's still the man of my dreams—and he's real. The reality, diminished though it is, is better than the memory and the dream. I have lost, but do not miss, my husband, he his wife. Does he miss her? Perhaps he too is a realist. In this matter, our bodies—unlike the mind clogged with fantasy—prefer realism. Our bodies are not fantasies, Mahmood's and mine.

"How about that!" exclaims Lucchesi as they pass the junk auto. He's entranced, halted at its rear by three shiny logos affixed to the trunk lid.

He says, "Wait. This is a Hudson? Or a DeSoto? Or a Studebaker?!"

"My research has yet to determine which. The ornaments for the boot were given to me as a girl by my grandfather, who drove such cars for play when he wearied of his Rolls Royce. This sad and horrible hulk was pulled from the river many years ago and left at the edge of my orchard. When my research determines the truth, it will be properly restored. The ornaments represent my yearning, Mr. Lucchesi, a homesickness. The pleasurable pain of needing to return. I can tell, as you say in your country, that we are on the same wavelength. I restore antiquities."

"You have homesickness for the pure American thing? Strange isn't the word. What does Mahmood think?"

"Mahmood thinks he is very much liking the present"—looking at Magda.

"And Ms. Cohen," says Lucchesi? "Where does Ms. Cohen stand on the desire for return?"

"Ms. Cohen desires to have such desire."

"We have not yet entered my home and we have already gone very far! Are you ready to enter, Mr. al-Sayyid?"

Mahmood is ready to enter.

Ruth would think of it—the room they sat in on that afternoon, darkness coming on—as a dimly lit museum storage space, bursting with a jumble of furniture from a mishmash of periods and cultures. Urns, jugs, cups, kalyx kraters, and looming in her memory, most of all, the funerary amphorae of classical vintage. Fans, screens. The photo of Hillary Clinton toasting Magda al-Radi. The smoking liquors of potent coffees and teas. Two and a half hours of free-flowing conversation, but fragments only of dialogue remain for her delectation—the sallies of Magda only, sutured to images of her husband and Mahmood stuffing themselves from an enormous tray of sweets.

Magda saying that the Tigris as it flows through Baghdad makes the shape of a double "S," like a long fat snake. That when her chickens ceased to lay during the Gulf War, she slaughtered them and fed them to the dogs, who would not eat them. That when it rains, it rains filth and there is no telephone service. That the sign of a truly caring and honorable father in Iraq is one who beats his children so badly they must be hospitalized, where they will be fed three meals daily, which he cannot provide. That Saddam is the hero of the Muddled East and Bush a dinosaur with the brain of a sparrow. That during the Gulf War her orchard was full of dead birds, and now with all the talk of renewed conflict, the birds have decided to die in advance. That Sunni Muslims believe all representations are an invitation to idolatry, so why does the Great Saddam, a Sunni, permit his picture to be taken, Ruth Cohen? That she awakes on many mornings to find the Tigris on fire and her kitchen full of dead flies. That Americans believe Saddam was responsible for 9/11 and Muslims that it was Sharon and the Jews of Florida—Americans and Muslims, a match of imbeciles, made in heaven. That her husband was shot to death in Basra while delivering a lecture on the extreme nationalism of the North Koreans. That all houses in the old quarter have secret underground passages for escape, including the house where you are staying, my friends, but where in Baghdad would you escape to? That Iraqi fundamentalists have weaponized their beards—this is the true meaning of the jutting fashion. They weaponize for the final jihad, making their beards more primitive than the infamous box cutters of 9/11. What can your Homeland Security do against the weaponized beard? That Mahmood cannot tell you when a sandstorm is coming because in Iraq weather forecasting is not allowed. That without culture life is unbearable. That before death one should take tea in the desert, in the transparency of desert light, to enjoy the crystalline clarity of objects. Because desert transparency is the only peace. That God is nearer than a man's jugular vein.

After Lucchesi had eaten the last three cookies, he checked his watch and said that he feared they'd overstayed their welcome. Ruth agreed, adding that tomorrow they have a long day. And Mahmood, eager to take them back, and more eager to return, agreed with guarded enthusiasm.

Magda replied, "Before you leave I would like to show you something very rare," and led them to the second floor, down a corridor on one side interrupted by a bedroom of ascetic simplicity, a study, a small library. The other side of the corridor is a dead wall, except for a single padlocked steel door. She turns the key and ushers them into a dark, windowless area covering one half of the upper storey. The massive drone of cooling and dehumidifying systems. She flips a switch and they are instantly gripped, as if unawares they'd come upon hallowed ground. Objects of varying size, some impressively large, hidden under black cloth. A heavy odor—what could possibly have produced it?—almost nauseating, recalling for Lucchesi the odor of the funeral parlor, with its banks of cut roses, as his mother lay cold and dumb.

She walks to the largest of the covered objects. They follow. With a flourish, she pulls away the black cloth, saying, "Voila! The first of my American antiquities."

A small but entire automobile, perfectly restored.

She says, "Do you recognize it?"

Lucchesi says, "A Crosley? They haven't been made since God knows when. How did you get it up here?"

"Piece by piece. I was hoping for a Nash Rambler."

She removes a second cloth. A miniature refrigerator, functional and running. She says, "Also a Crosley. Come. I shall take you to the lost world of our desire." A second refrigerator, it's a Kelvinator! with a 1952 calendar taped to the door. Lucchesi says, "I'm in love." A third refrigerator, an Admiral, alongside a television, console model: Admiral. Lucchesi says, "Oh, these names." She says, "Everything gleams." Runs her fingers across a Philco Duomatic washer-dryer. (Mahmood wants to run his fingers across her.) A cigarette cabinet: Old Gold, Pall Mall, Raleigh, Oasis. A detergent cabinet: Duz, Oxydol, Rinso White, Rinso Blue. A candy cabinet: twenty-seven boxes of Jujubes. A miscellaneous cabinet: a box of half-smoked Muriel cigars, a bottle of Good Old Guckenheimer Straight Rye, an Edsel trunk logo, a first edition of

The Great Gatsby, an unopened bottle of Coca-Cola, four bottles of Vaseline Hair Tonic, and a signed first edition of Rose Terry Cooke's breakthrough of 1891, *Huckleberries Gathered from New England Hills*.

Lucchesi says, "But Coke persists."

Magda says, "America persists."

Mahmood says, "But America will not always persist."

Ruth says, "I have not regained the lost world of my desire. Rose Terry Cooke?"

She unveils the last cabinet: A loaf, in pristine condition, of Velveeta Cheese, stamped Better if used before 24 Nov. 1964.

Lucchesi says, "How can it be?"

"I will tell you a secret. At Oxford, I did radical doctoral work on ancient Egyptian methods of corpse preservation. My thesis proposed a transition from preservation to actual revivification. Cheese, after all, is a kind of corpse. An experiment with a future, wouldn't you say? At Oxford I was considered dotty. Who's laughing now? The embalmment of Velveeta is a dramatic step toward the preservation of an entire culture, in the rich and radiant details of its everyday life. The book is completed. I call it, Paradise Regained. The Jujubes have been rendered immortal. Ecco, Velveeta! Do you believe that I have gone totally insane? Found putrid in my grandfather's freezer! Preserved! Restored! Edible!"

Ruth says, "You feel homesickness for a lost America? How is it possible? Good Old Guckenheimer?"

"I was taken to America as a child—where *I* was taken. My father had business in a very great American city. Where I acquired the Jujubes. Soon, back in Iraq, I developed with these items in my intimate possession a nostalgia for their place of origin. At Oxford, I made contact with a very special dealer in Sioux City. We are all Americans now. Stupid to resist. Cincinnati, my friends. My father took me to Cincinnati."

"There was a professional baseball park in Cincinnati," says Lucchesi. "Small, like that automobile there."

"You are going to thrill me?"

"And you can't bring it back."

He points to his head and says, "It's in here. It's better in here."

A hushed pause. He says, "What's in a name? If we have the name, we don't need the thing because we already have the thing. Everything is in a name. It was called Crosley Field."

Ruth says, "He has his own methods of corpse preservation—my husband is a novelist."

"And you, Ruth Cohen—are you not a photographer?"

IV

Larry

She'd written to tell me the procedure had gone smoothly, the defibrillator was working well, that she'd put the Adirondacks property on the market and was moving back to Utica, to 1311 Mary Street and the second floor apartment ("to be precise") in celebration of her husband's life. Would I have lunch with her? We'd toast his memory. (Had she closed the book on him?) She suggested we meet at The New Modernistic. Unbeknownst to her, the new owner—Charley's nephew's daughter—had thrown off the dead hand of the past and changed the name of the restaurant. It's now called The Modernistic, which is what it was called when Charley bought it from the Scala brothers, forty-five years ago.

Despite the long and largely personal conversation we'd had at the clinic two months ago, we found ourselves, once more, awkward and self-conscious—acting as if there was something between us. Over a decade ago, when Megan blew up, she said that she'd intuited something about me and Ruth on a deep level. Said I had something to answer for. Ten years is a long time—I felt that I'd moved on from whatever it was that my wife thought she intuited. It certainly wasn't what she thought, I could never agree to *that*, but I'll acknowledge (though not to her) that it was *something*. Sitting in the restaurant before her, I had to wonder if I'd moved on, or was just going to nurse forever the thing that glowed in some dark corner of my heart—I think of it more as curiosity than passion. Certainly not romantic passion. Call it passionate curiosity, if you like, and let's leave it at that—let's not call it romantic passion, unless you have a mentality similar to my wife's.

I sought refuge in small talk. Asked what she was going to do with the first floor apartment. (I can hear my wife say, She's going to rent it to *you*, Larry. Now that she's closed the book on him you have a clear shot at the grand prize.) She says, "I've rented it to a young Russian couple." I say, "Oh." She adds—in what I'd describe as a guardedly upbeat manner—that Aleksey and Natasha have ideas for the backyard and had asked her permission to plant tomatoes, start a grapevine, construct a trellis, and plant a cherry tree. Natasha's great grandfather had a cherry orchard in Russia. Ruth gave permission—gladly, she said. Because what they really wanted to do in the backyard, in her opinion, was plant a memory and watch it grow and bloom and bear fruit. She said, The fruit of a good memory is good living. A good memory has to be cultivated alongside the bad ones, which we assiduously cultivate, because it's hard not to—for balance, she said, we need to cultivate the good ones once in a while and not take them for granted: Because the good ones nourish the living in their struggle against the ghouls, who prefer that we dwell on the bad ones. I said, Sounds good to me, but hadn't a clue as to what she meant by the ghouls. She said there was a garden in the back when Thomas was a boy.

She wants to know why they changed the name of this place. Did Charley give permission? I had to tell her that a month ago Charley died. You wouldn't have heard, unless I told you. Which you didn't, she says. How come? I say, I guess I thought you had enough to deal with, considering. She says, Say no more. And we didn't. We ate in silence.

Then over coffee and cannoli, she says, I want you to know what happened. She tells me they were at the airport in Baghdad, awaiting their boarding call to Amman. They were to board in about twenty minutes, when he gets up and says, One more for the road. Be right back. He'd been to the restroom twenty minutes before, but was going to make another effort in the event they'd have to sit out on the tarmac for hours, buckled into their seats. You know all about his prostate problems, she said, but you don't know that the bastards took away his Flomax—that's the medication whose visionary name defines the last great hope of so many of my patients. He never returned. She barges into the men's room and is led away screaming by two men in black leather jackets, who force her onto the plane.

I remember a flight from New York once when the plane started to vibrate so violently I thought it was going to disintegrate in mid-air. That's what it was like watching her tell the story. Watching her slowly approach the shatter zone. I paid the tab and took her for a long walk. When we reached the rolling park on Utica's eastern edge, she'd gotten a hold of herself and said she was glad she'd told me the story—she needed to and had no one else to tell it to. She asked would I do her a favor. I said, Of course. Would I take her sometime to see Charley DiStefano, that's how she put it, because she didn't want to go alone, so that she could lay a single rose on his grave.

We strolled in the park, among the lovers in the grass. I brought up the republishing of *Cuban Stories*, which was having a big run, and in Utica was the talk of the town. She found herself suddenly famous again but had no interest and was turning down all requests for interviews, though some lurking photographer managed to snap her photo at Ninth Lake as she emerged from her cabin. The picture appeared last week in *The New Yorker*. If looks could kill. Publishers wanted to do a small book of her Saddam session and Susan Sontag had agreed to write an introduction. They were offering serious money. She said no. More serious after the no. Again no. When she delivered the film to *The New Yorker* and picked up the remainder of her payment she said the editor had difficulty restraining her glee upon hearing the news of Lucchesi's disappearance. The Knopf reprints of *The Prostate Dialogues* and his other two novels are being rushed through press and would appear next month. She said that the editor of *The New Yorker*, whose name she would not speak, and the head man at Knopf, whose name she could not recall, were two among the chief ghouls.

Just before we said our goodbyes, I mentioned the war in Iraq. Said I could not believe all that had gone on since she'd been there.

She said, "We're Jews together, Larry. Are we not?"

I say, "I'm drawing a blank, Ruth."

She says, "So what's not to believe?"

V

1311 Mary Street

In the summer of 2004—fourteen years, almost to the day, since she first moved to the house on Mary Street—she inhabits it once more, in his space now, on the second floor, waiting for the ghost who would answer the question he could not answer in life, when they strolled on Mary Street, fourteen years ago: "Will I be afraid?"

The resurgence of interest in her work is marked daily now by the thud of heavy packages hitting the porch below, as the mailman drops armfuls of what can't be stuffed into the box. Yesterday he'd let sail from the curb. How the house shook! Books from everywhere in the States and abroad, mailed in care of her publisher, or former agent, who forwards them to Utica. Obscure novelists, self-published memoirists, crank historians of the Middle East, small press lyric poets, the occasional literary scholar—all wanting to say how moved they were by *Cuban Stories*, how stunned by the photos of Saddam, how much they admire. Needing her to see their work (*see me!*) and perhaps write a brief note of acknowledgement, hoping that she'd experience a shock of recognition and assure them of their own ultimate value in the larger scheme of things, in the longed for appreciation of future generations. Think of Melville, she might say. Keep Melville always in mind.

Every two weeks she sends them, these unbidden gifts unread, to the underfunded public library, where they are promptly sold to a used book dealer for twenty-five cents each, who cannot sell them for fifty cents each, who deposits them, quite gently, in the city dump. Melville died in bitter obscurity, she might tell them, just as you will. For Melville's sake, and yours, we believe in the life to come.

The sounds on the porch below, at mail time, are the sounds of desire. Does he hear them? Lucky's work at last getting known. Does he weep for joy?

Today, a book from a photographer whose work she respects. Shots of nuclear sites in the American West. Ruth is absorbed, especially by this one—a vast flat, northwest of Las Vegas, bordered by two mountains named Skull and Little Skull. In the foreground: stubs of evaporated towers of concrete and steel, sand fused into glimmering glass by explosions whose centers were many thousands of times hotter than the surface of the sun. And in the middle and far distance, a prospect, somehow tranquil, of blackened soil peppered by Joshua Trees, re-emergent under desert haze and a pleasantly indifferent sky of baby blue. The photographer's notes tell her that Russian thistle (did he make it up?) thrives in the disturbed soil and that the site is known as Jackass Flats.

She looks up and says aloud, smiling, Do my ears grow long? She touches them, tugs gently, but the ghost will not respond. Recalls another photo, a favorite, in one of her dusty geological texts, of a thirty-year-old, wind-stunted limber pine, high up on a granite mountain dome in Wyoming, emerged from a tiny crevice, creeping a distance of twenty-three feet over the granite, and never rising more than thirteen inches in height.

Sounds of a creaking wheelbarrow, the chatter of those happy Russians working the back garden. They promise tomatoes in August. Soon she must plant bulbs of Autumn Crocus, so that she'll have white flowers out front in late September, just as they had always fronted the cabins at Ninth Lake, when the cold started to come on implacably. Autumn, he said, was the best time for his unavailable father. Time of the Fall Classic, when his father would say, "I have to discuss the World Series with my son."

She tiptoes onto the small back porch, gently opening and shutting the door: to peek down on the Russians digging in the garden and gaze down the backyards of Mary Street—imagining what he'd told her used to be. Clotheslines of vivid display, gardens and grape trellises as far as the eye could see, and The Tree, most of all the massive cherry tree of old Gregorio Spina, looming over the neighborhood like a guardian angel—gone, cut down by his Alderman grandson who blacktopped the backyard, the driveway, cut down the two maples in the front and blacktopped the strip of dirt between the sidewalk and street, where the maples once stood, in a line with the canopy of elms and chestnut trees of the 1300 block. All gone to blacktop. Aleksey and Natasha will maybe put these third generation aliens back in touch. A project of ethnic renewal. And should they fail? Eventually, Lucky said, the Bosnians are the saviors of lower East Utica. And if not the Bosnians, then the Vietnamese. And if not the Vietnamese? Some new group, some influx at sometime will eventually satisfy our nostalgia. They'll start in the corner of a yard, with the refuse heap of old kettles, old bottles, old rags, old iron—it'll start there. They will prove, Ruth, that in such foulness nostalgia ceases to look back and finds hope for the future.

In Winter, alone, and through early Spring at Ninth Lake, she'd let herself go. Had eaten too little, and badly, and lost weight. Her hair, always kept short, had grown to the shoulder.

One morning, on this street where she knows no one, strolling east toward St. Anthony Street, she notices a sign in a window: ANGIE'S HOME BEAUTY PARLOR. Knocks on the door and is greeted by Angie herself, who cuts her hair. And because Ruth is new to the neighborhood, Angie offers a manicure gratis. Ruth—who's never had one—accepts. Angie tells her that long ago there was another Angie who ran a beauty parlor in this very house, but her husband didn't go for it because the stink of permanents disgusted him, not to mention the hair on the floor in his kitchen. He was a stickler for sanitation. When they started to undergo marital discord, Angie decided to close the shop to smooth it out and not too long after they moved to Florida, where she wasn't too happy, but what could she do? He wanted Florida, which I could never see the allure. Angie's husband was a very good man, except when he showed his dictatorial streak. I'm telling you this story because you remind me of her a lot. Mind telling me your name, dear? Ruth said, Angie. Then Angie said, For God sakes I knew there was a reason you reminded me of her, and you'd remind me more if you kept your hair in a long style and put on a few, you really should, you know, because you got a hell of a frame that could accept it nicely.

Thereafter, when ever Ruth met anyone in the neighborhood,

she'd tell them her name was Angie. The ancient ones of Mary Street, hard of hearing, called her Ann, which she also enjoyed. And she let her hair grow to the shoulder again, which Angie the beautician preferred. Because the longer the better. Just like original Angie, said Angie. As was recommended, she put on a few and got back to her normal weight, and then she kept right on going. Ten more to be exact. The original Angie wore glasses, dear, and had a beautiful smile which you do too. But she smiled more than you. No offense. The optometrist insisted Ruth didn't need glasses, but she got them anyway.

She felt that she was acquiring some background. Some character. She was definitely filling out. The smiles come more frequently now, especially as she feeds the feral cat that haunts her back porch.

One day, Angie took her to a secondhand clothing store on Bleecker, where she (Angie!) found several of what they liked to call on Mary Street house dresses and two pairs of what the fashionable call mules, but which on Mary, according to Angie, are called a slide. A shoe without a back and a closed or open toe—like a slipper but more substantial, if you know what I mean. You can wear it on the street. You slide into it and you go out on the street to visit your friends. In appreciation for letting them have their way with the backyard, Natasha presented her with a traditional Russian shawl. Flowered, red roses on a cream-colored background and long black fringe. Angie took to wearing it over her head and shoulders whenever she went out for a stroll, which she did every morning after breakfast and in the early evening. They used to call it on Mary a walk around the block, even if you intended to go around several blocks. That's just what it was called. It was a big thing on Mary Street. A walk around the block. In late Summer and early Autumn they would see her, in her housedress, her slides, her shawl, her long hair and her new weight. Hello, Angie.

※

It's a cool day in October, at twilight, and Bleecker is unusually crowded, when Angie strolls by The Modernistic as Larry and Megan come from the opposite direction, hand in hand. She is wearing the shawl in the style she saw it worn in Iraq: over the head and around the neck. Just as they are about to pass with room to spare, a slight obstruction—a large man—causes Larry's shoulder to brush hers. His hand touches the hand of the shawled woman in the shadow of St. Anthony. Larry says, with a glance, "Excuse me." A few more steps and he and Megan approach the restaurant entrance. He halts. Megan says, "Something wrong?" He turns abruptly, casting a perplexed look back along the street, trying hard to catch sight of the shawled woman, but she—never glancing back—has already disappeared into the crowd.

Hearty thanks to William Noland—
creator of the real *Cuban Stories*.
And the late Nuha al-Radi.